The Anger of Aubergines

stories of women and food

BULBUL SHARMA

kali for women

women
UNLIMITED

The Anger of Aubergines was first published by
Kali for Women in 1997
This edition, 2005, by
Women Unlimited
(an associate of Kali for Women)
K-36, Hauz Khas Enclave,
Ground Floor,
New Delhi 110 016

Cover design: Sandip Sinha

ISBN: 81-88965-10-3

The characters in this book are imaginary.
If you see a reflection of someone you know, it is unintended.

Typeset at Comprint, B7-28/1 Safdrajang Enclave, New Delhi 110 029
Printed at Pauls Press, E- 44/11, Okhla Phase II, New Delhi 110 020

Contents

◆

Saying it with Cauliflowers

◆

Fenugreek, mustard, caraway, cumin and aniseed are thrown into hot mustard oil. A pungent aroma wrapped in smoke rises slowly, circles Dida's head and then travels towards us. My brother and I lean forward, taking care not to fall over the invisible line that divides my grandmother's kitchen from the rest of the house. No one is allowed into this tiny, dark room which is swabbed and cleaned four times a day by Dida. Onions, garlic, meat, glass dishes and servants have never entered the room, though a small brown mouse lives there and we see it sometimes, peering at us from behind a line of copper vessels.

Dida sits and cooks on the floor of the kitchen. I see her chopping vegetables into tiny pieces, cleaning rice, kneading dough or washing spinach leaves all through the day, although she eats only once a day and fasts every other day like all orthodox Brahmin widows. Sometimes my mother is allowed into the kitchen but only after she has bathed, washed her hair and changed into fresh clothes. Dida, who has always been frail and dressed in a widow's white sari ever since I can remember, cooks and eats before the other members of the family. The rest of us, her grandchildren, her sons, daughters-in-law and various poor relatives whom she likes to feed, sit around the long, marble table which Dida never touches—though she brought it with her as a child bride sixty years ago as part of her dowry. To her, it reeked of all the things she hated. Rich, red meat curries lashed with onions and garlic had stained it; at this polluted table her sons had entertained strange people who were certainly not Brahmins; and once she had seen a foul-smelling bottle of beer standing on it.

Dida liked to circle the table as we ate, and drop delicacies like fried aubergines, loochis and *mishti* onto our plates. She always stood a little away, taking care not to touch the table. Her pale hands, which I had seen her wash at least fifty times a day, would hover like dragonflies and then, suddenly, something delicious would fall on to our plates.

Dida was not much taller than me, then a 12 year old. She was so thin that the single gold bangle she wore often slipped off her wrist when she bathed. She wore no other jewellery except for this slightly dented, plain gold bangle because, she said, you must have one gold ornament on your body when you die, as a token fee for Yama, the God of Death.

"The priest will take it," said my uncle, who was an alcoholic and not afraid to talk back to her.

"Let him. Maybe he is the one to give it to Yama," she replied.

One of her favourite recipes was cauliflowers with *paanch phoron* (five spices), a delicate, pale gold, subtly flavoured dish. She would heap large amounts of cauliflower and loochis for each of us on a brass plate and slide it towards the door to her kitchen where we sat in hungry anticipation.

"Eat, eat. . . so thin you are," she would say as she watched us catch the plates like trained seals. Her simple food, without any garnish or colour, was always special because it was her way of caressing us without getting her hands polluted.

CAULIFLOWER WITH FIVE SPICES

1 small cauliflower, cut into sprigs
2 medium potatoes, cut into small cubes
½ tsp five spice mixture
(aniseed, cumin, caraway, mustard and
fenugreek seeds in equal quantities)
1 tbsp cooking oil
salt to taste

Heat oil in a kadai or deep pan. Add half a teaspoon of the five spice mixture. Let it hiss and crackle. Throw in the potatoes. Saute lightly. Add cauliflower pieces and salt and stir to mix the spices. Cover and cook on a slow fire for five minutes. Take off the cover and keep stirring often to make sure the vegetables are evenly cooked. They should be tender, yet firm. Serve hot with rice or pooris.

As for me, I can only claim to being an armchair cook, but I love collecting recipes. Some of the recipes in this book were Dida's and I'm sure she would be glad to know I'm sharing them with others. A few are successful recipes that friends, my mother and other genuine cooks have generously shared with me, and I'm passing them on. The rest are a few quick and lazy recipes I have cooked up myself while I wrote the stories.

I dedicate this book to my family and my friends for putting up with my burnt offerings. And I would like to thank Jaya Banerji for the brilliant title. Do try the recipes, though I must add that I take no responsibility for the results. You have been warned!

Bulbul Sharma
Delhi, August 1997

Jars of Gold

◆

BUAJI COUNTED TO TEN on her fingertips as she doled out the ghee. Each spoonful fell heavily like a clump of wet earth from a landslide and landed right in the centre of the bowl which the cook held tightly. Both of them watched the bowl and their lips moved in a silent count. . . seven. . . eight. . . nine. . . as the ghee hit the bowl with a soft thud.

Buaji was seventy-five and the cook a few months older. Both had slightly impaired vision but they never wore their spectacles when they encountered each other inside the storeroom. Each trusted their defective eyes more than any optical lens during this tense moment. Three times a day Buaji doled the rations out to the head cook with such meticulous care that not an extra grain of rice, sugar or dal ever entered the kitchen.

The storeroom was kept locked and the contents could

be viewed only for ten minutes, at six in the morning, eleven and then at four, like some rare, priceless exhibit on display at a museum. This was the only room in the huge, rambling house which had restricted entry and that is why it was held in awe and great respect by the family. They would stampede all over the corridors, crowd in the living room, sprawl in the many bedrooms but when they went past the storeroom everyone changed their pace. The men would walk past quickly to show they were not interested in the room. Unable to overcome a childhood habit, however, they would throw it a quick passing glance. The women of the house always tried to peer in surreptitiously, taking great care not to turn their heads a full ninety degrees. Family legend held that one of the tins was full of silver coins which Buaji kept hidden amongst the pickle jars. More than the silver I longed for the pickles that gleamed like gold mohurs in them.

Alert as an eagle on her nest, Buaji guarded this dark, narrow room with its polished red floor, its maze of shelves and a small window covered up with brown paper. Whenever the door was opened strange aromas escaped and floated all over the house. Once when I was ten, I tried to sneak into the storeroom but was caught at once in Buaji's steely grip. She held on to my plaits with one hand and continued to measure out the rice, uninterrupted, with the other. In the one giddy moment before I was dragged out, I caught a glimpse of a row of pickle jars glowing tantalisingly in the dim, brown-paper-filtered light. There was mango pickle in jaggery, a large glass jar of sweet and spicy cauliflower and carrot pickle, and next to that sat the pride of

Buaji's storeroom: ten little bottles of red chillies filled with spices.

"This girl will grow up to be a professional thief," Buaji warned my mother later that evening, when the family sat in judgement over me.

"She was only looking at . . ." muttered my mother.

"Looking? You know what looking with greedy eyes does to my pickles? They get mouldy overnight and die!" shouted Buaji. "These pickles know who is what and when it is the right time for them." And though confused by this statement, the family nodded eagerly. "If you touch them with soiled hands or at the wrong time of the month," she looked accusingly at the women who responded by blushing, "or if you think bad thoughts in front of the jars, they know it at once and the oil dries up and the spices turn bitter." We all looked guiltily away from the storeroom. "When I die you can have all the pickles and make yourselves sick." Buaji tugged gently at my plaits. The anger in her eyes had evaporated.

The pickles continued to simmer safely behind the locked door and only the head cook was allowed in twice a day when Buaji doled out the rations after counting how many people would eat that day. Children and servants were given half rations, the women a little more, while the adult men got full and generous amounts of everything. My father, who was her favourite, got not one but two plump slices of mango pickle, one piece of cauliflower, and sometimes a bonus spoonful of tamarind chutney. I would watch my father (who was an absent-minded eater at the best of times) while he ate, hoping he would not mix up the mango with the tamarind and ruin them both. As soon as he finished I would quickly pick up his plate and lick it clean on the way to the kitchen. Sometimes my father would give the mango pickle to my mother, though she never asked him for it, and Buaji would cough angrily.

Buaji had never been to school but was an expert at mental arithmetic—using only her fingers she could calculate the amount of ingredients required. In fact she was famous for her rationing skills and was often asked by relatives to dole out sugar, rice, vegetables and ghee during wedding feasts. The hired cooks would tremble when they saw her tiny, brisk figure and would flee, panic-stricken, to replace all the extra rations they had hidden under the kitchen table.

"Four spoons for Bannu and Mithu Bhaiya, two for the bahus, two for the children and three for 'you lot' in the kitchen," Buaji said in her clear, high voice, stressing the words 'you lot'. The cook shifted uncomfortably and then transferred his guilt by glaring at the young helper boy who was well known for his voracious appetite.

Buaji measured out the rice and sugar using a small silver cup which had been in the storeroom for more than thirty years. My father had drunk milk from it when he was a baby. Nothing ever changed its position in this room and even now, after so many years, when I shut my eyes I can see the line of biscuit tins, glass jars shimmering with precious pickles and sacks of flour slumped in their dark corners like a row of fat, dissipated bodies in a Roman bath. Some of the larger tins had English brand names from pre-war days and their faded labels with primroses and pretty blonde girls added a cheerful note to the gloomy room.

Buaji knew how much we longed to steal her pickles which she dispensed in such minute quantities to everyone except the men—so the storeroom had a huge lock. The key to the heavy brass lock was never kept with her main bunch of keys which hung at her waist. It was attached to a key ring, which one of her sons had brought back from a holiday in England, where it hung all alone attached to a shiny copper disc which said *Blackpool is Best*. The key was kept under Buaji's pillow at night and during her afternoon siestas.

One dark, summer afternoon, when the entire house was asleep, I, longing for bit of mango pickle, tried to steal the key. But my thieving heart froze when I saw Buaji's eyes. She was fast asleep. I could hear her gentle snores. But her half-open eyes looked straight at me.

I was not the only thief in the house. Once a month the household would rise in chaos when Buaji would wake up to find the key missing from under her pillow.

"Ungrateful wretches! Snakes I have fed milk! Thieves, dacoits, robbers! Devils who sell their own mothers!" she would scream and the servants, who knew at once it was them she was calling, would line up for inspection. For some reason they always chose to stand outside the storeroom door, probably to be close to the scene of crime which each one was certain the other had committed.

"Empty your pockets, each one of them. Even the secret thief's pockets you have inside your vests," Buaji would order as she marched up and down. I'm sure if she had a cane she would have tilted up the cook's chin with chilling firmness like a Nazi general in a war movie.

"Ma. . . leave them alone. . ." the sons would say and, without waiting for an answer, quickly leave the room. The women would form a circle at a respectful distance and watch.

One by one the servants would empty their pockets and I was always amazed to see what an odd assortment of things they carried on their bodies. Quickly, as if out of a magician's bag, would come out bundles of bidis, matchboxes (which Buaji would immediately confiscate, claiming them as her property), blunt penknives, buttons, bits of string and playing cards (which Buaji also grabbed, muttering angrily, "So that is where all your salary goes.") Soon the table would be cluttered with broken pens, pencil stubs, tiny combs, strange black pills, picture postcards of gods and movie stars, old letters and some precious documents wrapped carefully in plastic. Buaji and the servants were always astounded that the storeroom key was never amongst these meagre belongings. They looked at each other with renewed suspicion as if one of them had spirited the key away.

Then came Buaji's appeal to the gods in a shrill, complaining tone.

"O, Krishna! O, Vasudeva! O, Parvati Ma! Bless this house and make the thief standing here shamelessly amongst us, return the stolen item," Buaji never mentioned the word 'key' in her prayer because she felt that it was better to leave the field open for any other stolen goods to be returned by the gods.

The key would usually reappear by mid-morning just in time for lunch rations to be doled out. Peace would return to the house. The cook would laugh loudly in the kitchen and overcome with relief, slap the helper boys on their backs. Buaji never checked the contents of the pickle jars, tins and sacks in the storeroom because she was sure everything would be just as it was. The unseen hand that had returned the key would make sure of that.

MANGO PICKLE

1 kg raw green mangoes
1½ cups mustard oil
3 tbsp fenugreek seeds (methi)
4 tbsp fennel seeds (saunf)
2 tsp chilli powder
2 tsp turmeric
salt

Wash and cut each mango into four long pieces. Remove stone. Dry in the sun for two or three hours. Heat oil in a kadai to smoking point. Take off the fire and cool. Lightly crush fenugreek, mix fennel seeds, turmeric, chilli powder, salt and pour half the oil into this spice mixture. Put mango pieces in a large bowl and add the mixture to them. Use your hands to mix well so that each mango piece is covered with the oil and spice mixture. Transfer to glass or earthenware jars which have been sterilised. Pour over the remaining oil and tie a muslin cloth over the jars.

Keep in the sun for 4 to 5 days. Remove the muslin cloth and cover with a lid. Keep shaking the jar from time to time to mix the oil. Eat with parathas or pooris.

A Taste for Humble Pie

◆

BALA HAD COME TO stay with us after a long, exhausting round of various relatives. Each stay had taken another layer off the fragile dignity she tried so hard to preserve. But a perpetual smile, etched on her face like a birthmark, told everyone that Bala was a poor relative. Nobody in our vast, scattered family could remember how she was actually related to us but everyone called her by a name which declared some kind of relationship. I called her Bala masi; my little niece called her Choti Dadi to differentiate her from my mother; my uncles, who rarely ever spoke to her, called her Bala didi; but my father, for some odd reason, called her Bala bua, thus confusing the relationship further and giving it a faintly incestuous tinge. Bala answered to every name with a fixed smile and a slight tilt of her head to show that she was willing to do whatever was asked of her and also ready to accept that much was denied to her.

"I do not want it," she would jump up and say even before someone could offer her anything to eat, though people very rarely did. She lived with a minimum of needs, ate very little, never fell ill, never lost her temper or shed tears.

Though Bala had been around ever since I was a child, I could never remember her face when she was absent. Years of living with families who just tolerated her for her usefulness in the kitchen and her efficient nursing in the sickroom, had taught Bala to hover in the background, yet always be available. Wherever she lived, Bala could blend in with the family, unobtrusively.

When we sat together in the evenings, drinking endless cups of tea and catching up on family gossip, Bala always chose the most uncomfortable chair and sat on the very edge like a coiled spring, ready to jump up at a moment's notice if anyone wanted something—anything.

"Some salt. . ." my mother would say, not looking at Bala but at the ceiling, waving her hands in the air helplessly, but only Bala would run to the kitchen.

"Are the pakoras no good?" she would ask each one of us anxiously, as we ate.

Bala's pakoras were famous, better than anyone could make in the family, even my mother's, whose cooking was legendary. But I do not think anybody had ever told Bala how delicious her crunchy, yet light-as-air, pakoras were. She always looked so nervous when we bit into them. She had elevated pakora-making into an art and she surprised us with new flavours which made them taste totally differ-

ent. The pakoras were made with various vegetables. Sometimes she used finely sliced potatoes or thick, seedless aubergines. One evening, we would get paper-thin pakoras
made with spinach leaves and the next time our tongues
would be set on fire with green chilli pakoras, though Bala's
onion and cauliflower ones were her best. We usually had
these on rainy days but even if the sky had just clouded
over, we demanded them.

"Bala, pakoras!" we would shout and she would run
to the kitchen at once. Sometimes she used ajwain leaves
which tickled the tongue and added a sharp flavour to the
gram flour batter, or she would sprinkle poppy seeds on
spinach leaves before dipping them into the batter. Bala's
pakoras, though deep-fried in a large kadai of hot oil, were
crisp and crackling, never greasy, and we could eat as many
as we wanted without feeling guilty about straying from
our 'fat-free' diets. But I never saw Bala ever eat a single one
because she kept bringing them for us, running quickly
from kitchen to dining room and then back again to fry
some more, sweat running down her face and her breath
escaping heavily like a tail-ender in a hurdle team.

"You have some, too," my mother always said, with a
vague look at the plate now scattered only with crumbs,
when we had all finished eating. But Bala just smiled and
drank her tea which had gone cold as usual. "She likes it
cold. Always has," my mother would announce to whoever
cared to listen, and Bala always nodded eagerly.

Bala was not only a good cook and an expert at making
all kinds of unusual snacks which we enjoyed every evening,
she was also very skilled at mending and darning. My

mother and my sisters not only gave her all their torn sarees to mend but also collected a pile of old clothes from our other relatives for Bala to repair. I tried to protest once, though half-heartedly, because she was restoring my favourite old kurta, but my mother said, "Bala does not mind," and Bala, not looking up from her work, said, "I like doing it." My mother, annoyed with me for interfering, muttered in an angry voice, "Bala likes doing things for us. She is living here, isn't she? Just like a family member. I gave her a saree for Diwali, a pure silk one too, and you gave her your old handbag the other day. Bhaiya always remembers to give her something for rakhee. Bala is grateful and likes to be useful around the house, unlike some girls I know, who spend all day reading novels," she added, not missing her chance to get at me for upsetting her. Bala sat listening to us, smiling, as her fingers flew swiftly with practised ease.

My grandmother, who was the only one who remembered Bala as a young girl, hated to see her sitting down.

"Fetch my glasses," she would command as soon as Bala went anywhere near a chair.

"You have them around your neck, Bibi," Bala would point out.

"Then bring me my prayer book," Bibi would say, squinting with irritation. Bala always smiled and ran to fetch her book. "Not this one. The big one with the red cover," Bibi, who could not read, would say. Bala went back again, and they would carry on like this through the day, Bibi asking Bala to fetch and carry and Bala cheerfully carrying out her conflicting orders. The only time she was allowed to sit in

Bibi's presence was when she was either reading to her from the prayerbook or pressing her feet. They would huddle together then, Bibi stretched out on the bed, Bala kneeling on the floor at her feet, gently pressing the fragile bones.

"Mind you leave no marks. You know how soft and sensitive my skin is. Even a mosquito leaves a mark when it sits on me," Bibi said, watching Bala's hands as they moved gently along her feet. Then she would lie back, shut her eyes and begin to talk about long-forgotten family feuds which only Bala could listen to with such eagerness. Once in a while Bibi would mention Bala's parents, always with anger and spite and then Bala's face would transform fleetingly into another, almost a stranger's face. The fixed smile would disappear and her eyes would become alive with a curious kind of light, and for a moment she would look quite beautiful.

Bala's mother had died when she was a child and her father had married promptly, with shameless haste according to my grandmother.

"That rascal, with his henna-dyed moustache! He was already looking around for a new bride at his poor wife's shradh ceremony. With my own ears I heard him ask Kanta about her daughter. 'Is she the one who plays the sitar?' I heard him say, just as the priest was chanting the final prayers for the departed soul." Bala leaned forward to listen, her face bright with a desire to know more. "Press gently, *sarmunni*, you want to leave scars on me or what? Sitar. . . what did that rascal father of yours know about sitar music? All he knew was that he had got away with one good dowry and now had the chance of grabbing another one. Greedy swine, I call him," Bibi hissed. "I am not afraid of speaking ill of the dead. Bad blood stays evil. . . dead or alive, I tell you. Press on the other side now. Gently, you wretch," as Bala continued to stroke her feet.

Bala's father died soon after his second marriage, much to the satisfaction of all the righteously indignant relatives who flocked to his funeral from far and wide like gleeful, contented vultures. Soon after the funeral Bala's stepmother went back to her family, carrying her sitar with her, leaving Bala behind.

"We can get her married again to some widower but the girl will ruin her chances. Let her dead mother's family take her in," her family said before leaving, much to my family's anger.

"Who are they to advise us? Greedy hawks. Took every bit of jewellery back. Just left all the ill-luck that silly, sitar-playing bride had brought with her," they muttered. But the fact was no-one knew what to do with Bala.

"If she had been a boy it would have been so easy. Everyone wants an orphan boy. They are so rare and difficult to find," they said and looked at Bala with frowning impatience. They argued amongst themselves, bringing up past grievances against Bala's parents to justify not taking her with them, and the quarrels quickly became so bitter and personal that everyone forgot about her and plunged into raging battles. Soon they were not even talking to each other and an angry hush fell over the funereal house. Then finally one elderly aunt from her mother's family, worn out by the proceedings and eager to get back home, agreed to take her in. All the other relatives made up at once and went to the station in one solid flank to put Bala and the old aunt on the first available train, before she could change her mind.

Bala stayed with this old woman, looking after her till she finally died after a long illness, taking Bala's entire childhood with her. From then on Bala began her round of the various relatives, who bounced her back and forth like a football. She stayed for a while with us but then my father was posted abroad so she went to my mother's younger sister. But she was soon sent back.

"You know, we have a small house. I need that extra room where Bala is sleeping for my puja. It is not good to have the gods all cluttered up in one corner. What will they think of me," said my masi and Bala was shunted off to another family. After a few months she came back to us with a long letter of accusations against my father for shirking his duties, to which my mother sat down to reply at once while Bala was still waiting to unpack. Then she was packed off to an invalid widower uncle's house where the servants had all run away because my uncle had threatened to shoot them. Bala stayed with this cantankerous old man for three years, coping with his foul temper, pandering to his never-ending childish demands and accepting his callous, selfish treatment of her, as she learnt the art of being a poor relative.

Gradually, as the relatives grew older and Bala more skilled, they began to discover her hidden virtues. Besides being a good cook, she was found to be an expert at nursing the sick as well as a good manager of servants in the kitchen. The uncle who had muttered angrily, "Why should

I take Kanhu's child when he did not even have the decency to invite me to either of his weddings?" was now very happy with Bala.

"Just taste her pakoras—you will never find another one so delicious and crisp," he said but only when Bala was not around. To her face he continued to shout at her. Bala merely smiled as she ran about, deftly handling his conflicting orders, till he died suddenly, one day, with a plate of Bala's pakoras in his hands.

Unlike the time when Bala was a young girl, all the relatives now put in their bid for the '30-plus' Bala at once, and my mother quickly appointed herself Bala's manager. It gave her a great sense of power, especially over my father's relatives.

"Send Bala to us. My mother-in-law is bedridden," cried Phulo, my father's cousin. But my mother dismissed her claim, saying, "No, Bala should go now to Kusum chachi—she is bedridden as well as incontinent. Anyway, I do not like the way Phulo gave only Rs 101 at Bhaiya's wedding. Misers! Let them suffer. Bala will go to Kusum chachi," she said with a satisfied smile on her face and patted Bala's hands.

Bala, of course, had no say in the matter and would have been surprised if anyone had asked her where she wanted to go. She just waited to be sent wherever, her small suitcase packed and ready. Despite being suddenly so much in demand, Bala's attitude did not change. She still occupied the minimum space in the houses she was sent to and continued to wear her fixed, eager smile.

Though always polite and friendly, Bala never showed any special attachment to any one of us, or any thing, for that matter. Only once, when she was staying with us, did she get very fond of a mongrel puppy. She found it under the water tank in our garden and began to feed it scraps from the kitchen despite my grandmother's and mother's angry protests.

"There will be a pack of wolves soon at our door if this kind of thing is encouraged," my mother said to Bala; while Bibi, who saw bad omens in everything, from broken slippers to chipped teacups, added, "God knows where this wretched dog has come from, could be a bad omen. Why did it choose *our* water tank?" she asked Bala, eyeing her with suspicion. Bala continued to feed the puppy but now took care to hide the food in her saree pallav and take it out to the garden in the afternoon when everyone was asleep. One day Bala and I bathed the dog, using Bala's soap which she had sliced into half.

Since she never had any money Bala had to wait for my mother to give her things like soap, toothpaste and clothes. Her small suitcase was full of old hand-me-downs. Bala would wash and repair the old discarded garments and then, when she took them out of the suitcase, she would tell us the history behind each one.

"This blouse your mother gave me when she was nursing your brother. I washed all the milk stains away with hot water. Remember these red chappals? They were Kusum chachi's. Poor thing died before she could wear them out. This sweater is yours. You gave it to me just before you joined college," she said holding up the awful garment for me to admire.

Bala often rearranged the contents of her suitcase like

my mother did the drawing-room furniture. She took out each garment, examined it for any signs of wear and tear, which there always were, repaired them and then repacked them. She took hours folding each old blouse or sweater with loving care, smoothing the shabby clothes with affection as if stroking a child.

One evening she took out an old sweater, which was beyond repair even for her skilled hands, to cover the puppy. That is when Raj saw her for the first time.

"I told you that flea-ridden puppy would bring us bad luck," my grandmother would repeat every day after that fateful evening. Raj was a distant relative whom everyone in the family had forgotten till he suddenly arrived for my brother's wedding, rich and successful, bearing gifts from New Jersey. He saw Bala that evening as she fed the puppy, then tasted the pakoras she had made for tea, and from then on he began to woo her.

It was as if someone had thrown a huge stone into a calm pool of water. The ripples created chaos and the entire clan, even relatives who lived in far-off towns and only came to our house for funerals and weddings, were aghast at this development. My own family was thrown into a frenzy, and for once no one had anything to say because this unspeakable horror was taking place in our house. Raj followed Bala around the house, talking to her, trying to help with her endless chores, much to everyone's embarrassment. At first she was not aware of his attentions and thought he wanted her to do some chores for him, but she soon became suspicious when she saw that he never asked her to fetch or mend anything, he just talked to her in a soft voice. Bala was shocked and speechless with terror. She began to steal around the house trying to avoid him, hiding behind doors when she heard his footsteps. But Raj, who had built up a successful business of used cars from scratch with only a spanner he had taken with him from Ambala, was nothing if not persistent. He stood near the kitchen door for hours, nattily dressed and smelling of expensive aftershave, till Bala finally came out. He followed her to the terrace when she went to hang the clothes out to dry and sat with her when she pressed Bibi's feet, listening to her old stories and even adding some that he remembered from his childhood.

Although Bala had not spoken a single word to Raj, the family began to regard her with suspicion.

"Why did he pick on her when there are so many suitable girls of mature age sitting around waiting for grooms? It's not as if Bala is dazzlingly fair or beautiful," they whispered as she walked by.

"He has come from abroad," explained my mother weakly. She felt guilty because Bala had been in her charge and it was her duty to somehow smooth over this inexplicable happening. Though Bala tried her best to hide, she had suddenly lost her ability to blend into the background as she had done all her life, and now the family stopped and looked at her for the first time. Bewildered, her smile fixed like a grimace on her face, Bala crept around the house like a hunted animal. My mother thought of sending her away to some other town but there was the danger of Raj following her there.

"God knows what will happen if I let her out of my

sight," she said looking at Bala as she rubbed oil into my grandmother's hair.

"We have seen the shameless circus you have staged here by inviting strange men from abroad. They say he is a garage mechanic. How can we have a relative who does such lowly work? That, too, in America?" the old lady said angrily.

"Why? Your youngest brother was a taxi driver in the U.K.," my mother replied, happy to argue over a new issue other than the Raj and Bala episode.

Bala was now given more chores than before and she took shelter beneath piles of mending, making huge amounts of pickles, cooking, sorting out linen and reading tirelessly to my grandmother who no longer reprimanded her for leaving marks on her feet. Bala was now always accompanied by a bodyguard in the form of a stern, hawk-eyed relative. But instead of discouraging Raj's ardour it gave him a surge of energy and, like Sleeping Beauty's prince, he continued to hack his way through a forest of scowling relatives to seek Bala's hand.

Weeks passed and he made no progress. The family, somewhat less nervous now, knew all they had to do was hold the siege of Bala just a little longer, because soon Raj would have to return to New Jersey. Bala still refused to speak to him and when Raj, in desperation, finally asked my grandmother to intervene she snapped, "Why should I? No need for her to get married at this age." When he left she added, "I need her now. It's my turn. I'm the oldest and the sickest." Other relatives, keeping their increasingly fragile health in mind, and worried about a future without Bala looking after them, watched Raj with intense dislike as he tried to woo Bala.

"Wants her for his old age," they said disparagingly, shaking their heads.

"Must be the pakoras," my father explained.

One fateful evening, when Bala had been left unguarded for a moment, Raj followed her to the garden and proposed to her. My brother was sent out at once but he was too late. Raj had already stated his intentions and begged her to give an answer soon.

"What if she accepts him!" cried an uncle who had gout. Tension gripped the house once more. Panic-stricken, my grandmother cried, "Can't we show him someone else? Go find a girl quickly!" she ordered my mother. Like a magician, my mother at once pulled out a dozen marriageable girls of different ages. A surprised Raj was dragged to various houses where he drank endless cups of cardamom tea and ate lumpy cakes which proud mothers announced had been made by the girls with "their own hands". But Raj stayed faithful to Bala, though his time was running out.

"Why don't you get married to him?" I asked her one morning when we were alone, feeling like a traitor. Bala gaped at me, her eyes full of fear.

"Are you mad? How can I get married, ever? What will the family think of me?" she said and ran out of the room. Raj stood near the door with a bouquet of flowers. We knew the time of reckoning had arrived.

"Bala, if you agree to marry me, please accept these flowers," he said, his loud voice now reduced to a whisper. Bala stared at the bouquet, mesmerised by the flowers. The cellophane wrapping glistened and crackled as if the flowers were alive. A solid wall of relatives who had moved in closer, stood silently behind Raj, like Caesar's assassins, grim-faced and reeking of suspicious hatred. Bala moved forward and I held my breath. With trembling hands she took the bouquet, her eyes flashing, her smile strangely coy like a blushing bride about to garland her groom. Raj had just begun to smile triumphantly when Bala threw the bouquet back at him. I could hear the silent applause echo around us as the family realised their victory.

"I knew Bala would never let us down," said my mother later, when all was calm. "How could she, after all that we have done for her."

MINT CHUTNEY

Fresh green mint leaves
1 tsp amchur (dried mango powder)
pinch of salt
½ tsp sugar
1 green chilli

Grind the ingredients to a paste. Add 2 tsp yogurt mixed with 1 tsp water.

SPINACH PAKORA

1½ cups gramflour
½ cup water
½ tsp bicarbonate of soda
pinch of salt
¼ tsp chilli powder
¼ tsp pomegranate seed powder
3 tbsp mustard oil
spinach leaves, washed clean and patted dry

Sieve gramflour, soda bicarb, chilli powder, pomegranate powder and enough water to make a batter of coating consistency. Use your fingers to beat the mixture well, or if you are finicky, use a fork. Heat oil. Dip the spinach leaves one by one into the batter and deep fry in hot mustard oil. Place on brown paper to absorb excess oil, and serve hot with mint chutney.

You can add a variety of vegetables to this batter to make pakoras. Paneer cubes, cauliflower florets, hard-boiled eggs sliced into half, sliced aubergines, chunks of capsicum, whole deseeded green chillies and 'ajwain' leaves are my favourites. Fillets of fish and chicken pieces can also be made into pakoras but take care to slice the meat thinly and marinate it in a ginger-garlic paste before dipping into batter and frying.

Sandwiched !

◆

HE STOOD AT THE doorstep, reluctant to go in. He knew they would be waiting for him. They would be scanning the gate with furtive eyes, necks stretched forward, still as deer sniffing the air for the smell of danger. His mother would be closer to the door while his wife, just a few steps behind. As soon as he went in the battle would begin and the evening would be torn apart, like every other evening of his married life. Vinod, bowing his head low as if to make himself smaller and unobtrusive, stepped into the house. His mother lurched forward from her vantage point near the doorway. She was holding a glass of juice today. The red liquid glistened like freshly drawn blood in the frosted glass and Vinod felt a sudden wave of nausea.

"It is phalsa juice, beta. I made it just now. Gives you strength," she said, pushing the glass into his hands with a triumphant smile because today she had got him first.

Nirmala, his wife, stood hidden behind the curtains and he could feel her anger seep through the flowery pattern of the cloth. He could hear the tinkling of her bangles and knew she carried a cup of tea in her hands. Vinod shut his eyes as his taste buds recoiled with the memory of Nirmala's tea. The peon in his office, the dhaba boy, a railway tea-stall, even a hospital kitchen could not make tea taste as terrible as his wife could. Sometimes Vinod marvelled at how she consistently managed to concoct tea that was both bitter and watery, full of curdled milk and lukewarm. Yet he always smiled when he swallowed it day after day. A broad grin somehow helped to relax his throat muscles which always clamped shut when he took the first sip of Nirmala's unforgettably unpalatable tea.

Vinod finished the phalsa juice, draining the last sour drop under his mother's unwavering, watchful eye, and then went forward to tackle his wife's tea. His stomach somersaulted inside him, his body stalled like an alarmed mule, but like an automaton, Vinod reached out for the waiting cup. He ordered himself to smile, held his breath and gulped the ashen liquid down, never taking his eyes off Nirmala's face. How beautiful she was and how much he loved her, he thought, as he felt the tea travel down his throat, tannin leaving a trail of bitterness which would last till dinner.

He did not want to think about dinner as yet. There were still a few hours of peace left till they took up their positions for the next attack. His mother had gone into her room but had left the door open. That meant she wanted Vinod to go and sit with her this evening. It also meant that

Nirmala had once again broken the rules and stepped out of her circle into her mother-in-law's territory.

"You know I never want to interfere," began his mother with her usual opening lines, "but at my age I deserve some peace and quiet. I never ask for anything, you know. That is my nature. . .your father also knew it. 'She never asks for anything,' he always used to say to his family. But that does not mean that everyone has to treat me like a servant. Does it?" she asked Vinod, her eyes sparkling with anger.

Every time she got angry, Vinod saw his own features take over her face. Her skin lost its dry, transparent texture and began to glow with a dark, mottled sheen. Her mouth, usually set in a thin, delicate line, now looked jagged and masculine.

"She is only 54. If she were European she could have married again. . . though now even Indian widows. . ." Vinod shook his head to stop thinking about what could never happen.

"Have you got an earache? I knew you would, after eating that ice-cream she made. Just water and colour it was. I am surprised you are not coughing as yet," she said, raising her voice.

"No, Ma, I'm all right." He suppressed a sudden urge to cough and sat still, trying to look attentive. His mother began to talk in a low voice, looking at the door at the end of each sentence. She knew Nirmala was listening and raised and lowered her tone tantalisingly, whispering bits of information one moment and complaining loudly the next. "What is the need for taking an extra kilo of milk when her friends come? Are they lactating mothers that need so much milk in their coffee?" she asked. Vinod knew that the guests desperately needed the extra milk because Nirmala's coffee was a shade worse that her tea. He remembered fondly how he had choked over it when he had gone to see her during the negotiations for their marriage. . .

"Nirmala has made everything today," her mother had proudly announced. The shrivelled samosas, disintegrating gulab jamuns and lethal coffee, were all Nirmala's creations, and Vinod ate everything that was offered to him like a starving man because he had already fallen madly in love with Nirmala and the food was nectar to his lovesick taste-buds. Vinod glanced at his watch surreptitiously and saw that there were still five minutes left for this tirade to end. His mother never continued beyond 6:30 which is when her favourite T.V. programme began. She was now hastily winding up what she had prepared to say and talked so fast that she ended with two minutes to spare. They sat together in awkward silence for a while and then his mother dismissed him by saying she had to go to the bathroom.

Now it was Nirmala's turn, but Vinod did not mind his wife's counter-accusations because he could stroke her arms and kiss her fingertips while she talked. But today for some reason she was not as animated in her attack as on other evenings, and spoke with a listless air as if she was complaining because it was expected of her.

"Are you not well?" he asked solicitously, touching her forehead.

"No, I am fine. Just a little tired. Your mother rubbed some oil in my hair in the afternoon but she kept scolding me so much I could not go to sleep after lunch. I have made a new chicken dish for you. I saw it on the Zee T.V. cooking programme. . . it's from Italy. The electricity went off in the middle of the programme but I knew what the man was going to do."

Vinod sighed, but told himself dinner was still two hours away. So many things could happen by then. There could be an earthquake if he was lucky; he could be called to the office on urgent work; some guests might drop in and he could insist on getting take-away food; they might run out of gas; or he might even get a mild heart attack and be put on a glucose drip. But the evening passed like a flash of lightning and time for dinner arrived, as it did with un-failing regularity at the end of each day.

From the day he had married Nirmala, Vinod had been facing this battle for his palate and had wearied of it. The women prepared a new strategy each day. Sometimes they fought with curries, each one producing a more spicy, more fragrant, hotter version which set his mouth on fire and gave him nightmares. If one made a rich red Roghan Josh swim-ming in fat, the other produced a kofta curry with a thick almond gravy. When his wife placed before him a dish of Butter Chicken which looked as if the chicken had been dipped in orange dye, his mother would counterattack with meat balls drowning in a lake of yellow ghee. If one made reshmi kebabs tough as jute rope, the other quickly brought forth pasanda kebabs, stiff and dark as pieces of ebony. Both were bad cooks who needed to be praised for every mouth-ful that choked him. Vinod often wished he could divide his body vertically into two equal parts and give each portion to each woman. He wanted so much to please both.

Nirmala knew that her mother-in-law was a better cook because she had had an earlier start on feeding Vinod and knew exactly what he liked. But she was catching up by reading cookbooks all day. She made copious notes in a diary which she consulted every time she cooked. She held the battered diary—it had fallen many times into the spice tins, had gravy stains and a singed corner—in one hand while she cooked. Ever since she had seen the old lady flipping through her precious diary one day, she kept it locked up in her cupboard. A few more months of practice and Vinod would be eating out of her hand, literally. If only her phulkas could be perfect spheres like his mother's were, instead of a series of misshapen blobs which were a source of endless humiliation.

Her mother-in-law always laughed softly when Nirmala placed the scarred, deformed phulkas onto Vinod's plate.

"What rubbish this girl produces despite her convent education and fluent English," thought Vinod's mother. "It's not enough to have fair skin and a pretty smile to keep a man happy. He needs food, too." *She* did not need a book to tell her how to cook. Her mother had taught her everything when she was a young girl and though they had many servants, she always cooked all her late husband's meals. Even on the day he died he had eaten a full plate of methi alu, four paneer parathas, a big bowl of kheer and two laddoos she had made with pure cow's milk ghee from their village. Vinod, too, loved her food. As a child he would rush to her at mealtimes and demand to be fed first. She would break a hot paratha on a plate and mix it with gravy, add a big blob of white butter and roll the mixture into tiny round balls. These she would drop deftly, one by one, into his mouth, opened wide like an ever-hungry fledgeling. Now it broke her heart to see him gulp down his wife's foul food, which even the servant boy could not eat. She longed to snatch it away from his hands and throw it into the dustbin.

"She always pushes her own dish in front of you and that is why you do not eat what I have made," Nirmala would complain. "She locks the kitchen door when she cooks so that I can never see what spices she has put in the curry. Don't blame me if she gets burnt in the kitchen one day and can't be saved. It will serve her right. She can take her secret recipes to heaven with her." Nirmala would mutter in their bedroom after she had presented yet another failure for him to choke upon and praise lavishly.

For the last one week he had noticed that now they not only fought over curries but had extended battle lines to puddings, too. Here, Nirmala was beginning to get an edge over his mother because her cakes were surprisingly good while the old lady could make only kheer and halva. Then last week his mother changed her tactics and upstaged Nirmala. She now waited for him each evening with a new kind of juice in her hand. Sour fruit juices, strange smelling thandai, gritty jal jeera now welcomed him home. These lethal red, green and brown beverages were also accepted by his helpless stomach where kheer already clashed with carrot cake and heavy curries sat all night like demons made of stone.

Some days were so rife with battle cries that his skin would erupt in a fine pink rash. But he never fell seriously ill. Each day Vinod ate what his mother had drowned in ghee, and his wife's burnt offerings. His digestion accepted it bravely and stoically. Sometimes he wished he would come down with some disease which would put him on a restricted diet and force the women to call a ceasefire. Then maybe they could become good friends because they were really quite fond of each other when not competing to feed him. Nowadays everyone he knew had ulcers, blood pressure or was dangerously overweight, but his stomach never protested beyond an occasional, mild grumbling and a few loud belches. He remained cholesterol free, had normal blood pressure and was as slender as a reed.

As soon as he sat down at table, his mother leapt up to put a large spoonful of til alu on his plate, next to the tomato rice. Nirmala retaliated by covering it up with a dollop of Pollo Firenze.

"Not so much, please," he said, looking at neither of them. His every refusal, acceptance or praise had to be equally divided between them. Vinod had perfected the art by looking directly at his father's portrait which hung above the dining table every time he spoke.

This evening Nirmala seemed a little distracted as if she was participating in the food race just by force of habit. He could tell by her somewhat slow, lethargic gestures when counter-serving his mother's helpings, that her heart was not in it.

"Are you not well?" he asked her again and his mother, too, stopped heaping rice on his plate to look at her.

"I'm going to have a baby," Nirmala announced and burst into tears.

Vinod rushed to her and caught her hand. His mother began to cry, too, but smiled happily at them as she wiped her tears with her saree.

"Lord Krishna. . . you have answered my prayers. . . bless this girl, lord, protect her from the evil eye," she said. Her hands quickly circled Nirmala's head and she cracked her knuckles at her temples. Nirmala took her cue and bent down to touch her feet.

"No. . . no. . . you sit still. . . you must take care of yourself now. The baby must be born healthy. I will make panjiri on a candle flame. It will make you produce milk. You must be three months gone," she said giving Nirmala a sharp look, like a farmer assessing his prize milch cow.

Nirmala answered at once, looking more alert and cheerful.

"We can always give him powdered milk if I do not have enough milk. Then Farex. . ."

"What! Feed my grandson from a tin! Never! I will get cow's milk for him, fresh white butter, curds. . ."

"Everyone gives eggs and cereal now when the baby is three months."

"That is why their teeth fall out when they are thirty. Look at Vinod, how healthy his teeth and bones are," said his mother and both the women turned towards him. But they seemed to be looking beyond him at a child who was not yet born. A child they would compete with greater joy to feed.

Vinod felt their indifferent gaze wash over him like a breath of cool, fresh air. He knew he was a free man. There would be peace at home for the next six months and then they would again do battle, but this time it would not be over him. Vinod wished with all his heart for a healthy, strong son because a daughter, however precious and loved, would not be distraction enough.

TOMATO AND GREEN GARLIC RICE

1½ cup long grained basmati rice

3 large tomatoes

2 medium onions

1 tsp fresh garlic paste

2 tsp green garlic leaves finely chopped

5 tbsp oil

1 tsp chilli powder

1 tsp coriander powder

1 tsp mustard seeds

2 tsp black gram dal

2 tbsp roasted peanuts

a few curry leaves

salt to taste

Blanche and puree the tomatoes. Add enough water to make four cups of liquid. Pour it in a vessel and add the rice along with the salt. Cook on slow fire. While it is simmering, in a separate vessel, heat the oil and fry the mustard seeds and black gram till the mustard starts spluttering. Add peanuts, curry leaves, garlic and garlic leaves and the chopped onions to the crackling mixture. When the onions turn brown add coriander and chilli powder. Fry for another minute and then add to the rice—take care because the mixture will splutter when it hits the simmering rice. Cover and cook till the rice is soft. You can eat this lovely orange-coloured, tomato-flavoured rice just by itself or with yogurt raita.

CARROT CAKE

400 gms flour

350 gms caster sugar

1½ cups peanut oil

4 eggs

2 tsp cinnamon powder

2 tsp baking soda

1 tsp salt

3½ cups grated carrot

200 gms chopped walnuts

100 gms raisins/dates/sultanas

Take a big bowl. Put all the ingredients into it and mix with a strong wooden spoon. The mixture will be sticky and difficult to stir. But don't worry. Bake in a large, greased, floured cake tin for 45–60 minutes. It is always surprising to see the gooey mixture transform itself into this attractive, cinnamon-flavoured, pale orange coloured cake. Ice using recipe below. If you are strong-willed, store in the fridge for two days before eating, to allow time for the flavours to develop.

SOFT CHEESE ICING (Optional)

25 gms icing sugar
50 gms melted butter
½ tsp vanilla essence
200 gms yogurt to make soft cheese

Hang up the yogurt in a muslin cloth. A couple of hours of draining will give you about 100 gms of soft cheese. Beat the cheese with the rest of the ingredients and ice the cake. Or, if you don't want to ice the cake, add chopped mangoes, peeled oranges or any soft fruit of your choice to the soft cheese and serve chilled as a dessert.

PHALSE KA RAS

½ kg phalsas
sugar to taste

Wash fruit in running water. Sprinkle over with 3-4 tablespoons of sugar (or less, if phalsas are especially sweet). Gently rub sugar into fruit until well blended. Place this sugared mixture in a pan and cover with 2 glasses of water. Strain through muslin, gently squeezing to get every last drop of juice. Remove the mashed up fruit mixture and pour another two glasses of water into it. Repeat the straining and squeezing process.

The result will be a clear, wine-red juice, piquant, delicate, extremely cooling and delicious.

Feasting with a Vengeance

◆

THE CROW FLEW OFF the tree and landed near Srilata's feet. They looked at each other for a moment, two pairs of sparkling, angry black eyes met, and then before Srilata could cry out, the bird gave a low chuckle and flew away.

"It is cursing us. I tell you, Mr Verma, it is a bad omen. The girl will be rejected again," she said and heaved a long sigh of resignation before lifting her cup of tea once more. Her husband continued to read the newspaper but a slight shake of his knees showed her that he had acknowledged her remark. So she continued, "There are so many ugly women married to perfectly good husbands. It is not that our Preeti is ugly, only her skin is a little dark. See—her nose is perfectly straight. Her eyes are big and her teeth, now that the braces have come off, so well aligned. Cost us 7,000, but well worth it. Though I still think that dentist chap over-charged us. Your sister's nephew he is, but who cares for family ties anymore." She paused to look at her daughter who was eating a toast with total concentration, her perfect row of teeth biting into the soft, white bread with relish. Her mother sighed once more.

Preeti was 24 years old and still unmarried. Her height, weight (slightly modified), colour of her skin, caste and educational qualifications were condensed into one crisp line—

24/160cm/59kg/B.A./wheatish/Khatri

—and advertised each Sunday in the local daily, but so far not one suitable boy had come forward. The postman did bring a bundle of letters each morning and Srilata, waiting at the garden gate for him, pounced upon them, but not one letter was from a 'status' family which matched the Verma's position, wealth and caste. One or two rare candidates who were found suitable did not carry forward the negotiations after they saw Preeti.

"We don't like those who like us and those we like, don't like us," explained Srilata to her relatives each time they asked when Preeti was getting 'settled'. Mr and Mrs Verma would carefully read the letters that arrived and then Mr Verma would put them in a leather-bound file, pasting the passport- size photographs with each letter. Preeti was never shown these letters. "Just in case she gets the wrong idea and selects some fortune-hunter whose photograph appeals to her," said Srilata. But every afternoon, when her parents took a nap, Preeti opened the file and studied each photograph with interest. She preferred the black and white ones to the glossy, coloured pictures because in those the blurred grey-white eyes of the prospective grooms looked kind and full of hope.

"Maybe we should increase the size of the ad. Take a few inches more space. Then maybe better families will reply and not all these lower middle class types we have received replies from so far," Srilata wondered loudly not expecting an answer from her husband, but he suddenly lowered his newspaper and said, "I am not taking a bigger ad. We have spent enough money already. Are all these boys' parents blind or illiterate that we have to spell out the words for them in bold typeface? Why not advertise on the radio then? What about the T.V.? This is the last Sunday I am repeating the ad."

Preeti wiped her fingers on her kurta and reached for another toast.

"Stop that. Can't you use the napkin?" said her mother irritably. "Anyway, you have had enough toast. Look how fat you are getting ever since you left college. Just sitting and watching T.V. all day or talking on the phone. What was the point of sending you to that slimming place? Are you using the Shafair I got for you? And what happened to your music teacher? I am so fed up of you and your father . . ." Srilata suddenly broke off in mid-sentence and looked up at the tree. The crow had returned and was once more preparing to land at their feet. It stretched its neck forward and gave a low chuckle, looking directly at Srilata as if challenging her, and then began to descend. Srilata got up from her chair with a loud war cry and began to furiously wave a white napkin at the bird. Preeti thought she looked like a stranded sailor hailing a passing ship. The crow had now settled down near the table and Srilata, afraid to go too near the bird, was screaming abuses at it from the other side. Preeti seized the opportunity to grab another toast. As she chewed contentedly, she looked at her hands, plump and dark, and wondered what there was for lunch.

The week passed but no replies were received to their last and final call for a groom.

"The boy does not know what he is missing," said Srilata. "He will get a car, a flat, shares in the best companies and membership to the most select club in Delhi. It is a pity we cannot say all that in the ad. Everyone is so secretive about giving a dowry and all. In my time my father displayed each and every item he had given Mr Verma, along with the price tags. 'Let everyone see. What we are giving, we are giving. No secrets,' he had said and people were amazed at the huge quantity of things I brought with me. Just for the maids my mother had given 51 suits, so you can imagine what the rest of my in-laws got. But, of course, they were never grateful. To this day they use the crockery given by my father but not one one word of thanks have I ever heard." Srilata cast a quick glance at her newspaper-camouflaged husband. Her friend, Mrs Chawla, who had dropped in for tea, nodded her head and pretended to listen carefully though she had heard the dowry story many times. She waited patiently for her turn, when she would talk about *her* wedding feast which had lasted for three days. They often had this conversation and both enjoyed it. But her chance never came because Srilata was called away to the phone. When she came back her face was flushed and she was breathing heavily.

"Is it bad news ?" Mrs. Chawla asked and leaned forward eagerly, rearranging her features to show horror or sympathy at a moment's notice.

Srilata pulled the chair out slowly and sat down as if in shock. She did not say anything and now even Mr Verma began to look interested.

"God does everything in his own time," said Srilata, and paused. "He waits and watches, waits and watches and then he does what he has to." Mrs. Chawla listened in silence, nodding at the right places. She did not want to interrupt her friend because she knew there was some news of great import which needed these rhetorical introductions before being announced.

"I thank you in heaven, my late father, without whose blessing this could have never happened," Srilata said and they both looked up at the clear blue sky. Mrs Chawla even saw a face in the cloud and she pointed it out to her friend. Srilata took a deep breath and Mrs Chawla held hers. Mr Verma looked at his feet. The moment was ripe. . .and then Srilata burst like a dam.

"A boy! A boy has been found. . . has selected our Preeti," she said, her voice trembling. "And what a boy. 175 cm /M.B.A/15,000 and fair, too. Not our sub-caste though, but who cares for these things now. It is the fruit of my good deeds in my last life. Oh my god, bless my girl!" she said and burst into a flood of tears.

Preeti was surprised to find that the boy was actually quite pleasant to talk to. They had met before at a cousin's wedding but she had only seen him from afar. Their respective parents had circled each other like boxing partners, each wary of making the first move. She wondered why he had agreed to marry her. "Must be exhausted by his parents like me and wants to get it over and done with," she thought.

Manu wondered if the girl's family knew he had been married before.

Innocent divorcee/judge for yourself

had announced the ad his parents had given, much to his embarrassment.

"We must tell the truth otherwise, later, there could be problems. Why do you feel so ashamed?" his father had asked. "What is wrong with getting married through a matrimonial advertisement like this? We have seen what happens when you find you own bride. Love marriage and all. She ran away with your best friend. It would have never happened if you had let us check out her family background."

"Her father is a supreme court judge," Manu said weakly.

"So what? There are judges and judges. We could have checked him out. Asked your mother's cousin who is a lawyer. Anyway, that is over and done with. Now you see this girl. She is a little plump, not very fair, but from a very respectable family. Only daughter. Father owns extensive property in South Delhi, farm, factories. Early marriage." His father spoke in shorthand like a matrimonial column advertisement.

Then began the actual bargaining.

"The boy's side have no demands but she is our only daughter. After all, this wealth is for our children, no? We cannot take it all with us," her mother said to the relatives, who smiled politely. Later, Preeti heard them whisper, "They have bought a boy for her. A second-hand one at that."

She did not mind. She was happy to see her mother laugh like she used to when Preeti was a child and they played hide-and-seek together in the garden. Her father seemed less sullen and came out from under the newspaper more often. In fact he had even smiled grimly at Preeti at the breakfast table once, which almost made her spill her cup of tea. Her mother no longer paced the terrace every evening, wringing her hands as she rubbed cold cream on them, muttering, "What will happen to the girl when we die?"

Preeti had never thought much about her future, which seemed blurred and beyond her control anyway, and probably very much like her present. But sometimes when the house was quiet and she was alone in the afternoons, she felt a sudden dart of fear about marrying a man who had spoken to her only twice. Then she quickly opened the boxes of new sarees which were piled up in the guest room. As she touched the smooth tissue paper, stroked the zari pallavs and traced the paisley patterns, she would begin to feel much calmer and would spend the rest of the day happily arranging the new dinner set, silver and linen. It was just like playing with dolls and the future seemed quite safe and familiar.

The priest fixed an auspicious date and suddenly the

house was full of relatives who arrived from various parts of the country, loaded with bedding and suitcases as if they meant to stay forever. Every corner of the large house was turned into a makeshift sleeping area and it soon began to resemble a refugee camp. Men sat drinking tea with Mr Verma and listened attentively as he read aloud bits of interesting news from various magazines and newspapers. The children played noisy games in the garden while the women divided themselves into two groups. The older ones combed each other's hair while they talked about other weddings they had attended and made surprise visits to the kitchen to check on the servants; the younger lot went shopping with Srilata, then spent the rest of the day examining the dowry in detail, for faults. A smell of rich food rose from the kitchen all day and filled the rooms, as the vast extended family were fed like babies every hour. Preeti, for once, did not feel like eating though she watched the halwai spread out his freshly made sweets every morning.

"No food from hotels. We will call our old halwai and he will cook in front of our eyes every day. I want to see what we are getting. No stale food hidden under fancy carrot and beetroot flowers for my daughter's wedding. Only pure ghee," her father said briskly, and Preeti had never seen him look so animated. He now sat in full view, not hidden behind his newspaper, every morning and held court in the middle of an admiring grove of relatives. He talked about his own wedding and lamented the present trend in hotel weddings.

"They serve salads now. In my days only the groom's horse was given carrots. We were a hundred and twenty men in my barat. How my wife's family gaped at us, dumbstruck. They barely managed to feed us. No women were allowed in the barat but now you see them not only in the barat but also dancing shamelessly on the streets." Everyone clicked their tongues in polite agreement.

Srilata, too, held her own court. Here, relatives were given her view of the same wedding held 30 years ago.

"They came like hungry hordes. Luckily my father had made perfect arrangements so we could handle the crowd. They ate like beggars and then demanded baskets of sweets for the people who could not come for the barat. My father gave them enough sweets to last a month. The whole town talked of my wedding for years. My mother gave a silver coin to each barati and, imagine, some of your father's baratis had never seen one before." She laughed and playfully pinched Preeti's cheeks. The relatives smiled on, munching happily on the crisp kachoris the halwai had just fried in a huge cauldron.

"Thank god a boy has been found at last for Preeti," they said. "Even though he is a second-hand one," they added in a whisper and looked at her with new-found interest, as if a miracle had occurred to change her into a strange, new being.

"God be thanked again and again. Otherwise her fate would have been like Gauri's daughter," commented one old aunt. "Remember the one with that ugly mole on her cheek? Gauri died last year and the girl is all alone now, in that big house. I hear she keeps stray dogs and roams the market in an old housecoat. So sad. How rich Gauri was. With servants in uniforms and white lace napkins on her table. She even spoke in English to her dog." Everyone fell silent and shifted uncomfortably as the plate of kachoris grew cold on the table. Preeti wondered if she, too, would have roamed the streets in an old housecoat if this boy had not agreed to marry her. She felt a sudden surge of anger against him but she could not remember his face. She reached for a kachori and all the relatives quickly did the same.

"What misers! Imagine calling a halwai. They can easily afford to hold the wedding in a big hotel. Hope the father is not going to be difficult with money," complained Manu's father as he sipped his tea with loud, irritated slurps. "We can look elsewhere. There is still time."

Manu looked at his mother, hoping she would take up the argument on his behalf this morning. He was tired of it all and just wanted the wedding to be over. He did not care anymore who the girl was or what the father did or served or ate.

"What about that family from Ambala? The one with the fruit pulping factory?" he asked his wife. Manu's mother looked at him in silence and then folded her hands and shut her eyes as if in prayer.

"Durga ma, give this man some sense. Help us, mata. Give me the strength to bear with this," she said, her eyes shut. "Listen, this girl is our final choice. They are a good family and Manu will be safe with a plain and simple wife. No more beauty queens for him. One divorce is enough in our family. You want to be like Kapoor uncle? He has spent 10 lakhs in the last two years on his two sons' weddings.

Each one of them has been divorced and remarried twice. He could have kept that money in fixed deposit and earned a good return by now," she said. "And remember how big the Ambala party girl's ears were? You only said the entire family had ears like that. It was some hereditary defect, you said. I like this girl. She looks dependable, not the run-away type. So forget about your greed for more money. And don't keep circling around their house like a burglar on the prowl. You think they cannot recognise you just because you are wearing that silly cap. Stop being a Sherlock Holmes and go and get the wedding reception details organised." She put her teacup down firmly on the table. Manu quickly finished his tea and left. He could hear his father still grumble on about the halwai, but his mother had walked away.

Now that there were only five days left for the wedding, a fierce competition began between both 'parties', and since most of the guests were common to both, each side tried its best to outdo the other. Manu's father became more and more agitated because Preeti's father seemed to be getting the upper hand in this battle of feasts.

"You know, they got their halwai all the way from Amritsar. That man has magic in his hands. The rajkachori and alu Amritsari he made last evening I will never forget," said one guest tactlessly as he sat down to lunch at Manu's house.

"Well, we are the boy's party. We do not really have to do anything, but since Manu is our only son we, too, have organised a party tonight at *Rendezvous Resorts*. It is costing me Rs 25,000 plus taxes, but what is money where your son's happiness is concerned," said Manu's father.

"And especially when it is the second time around. Double expenditure for you, too," added the guest helping himself to large piece of chicken. Manu's father hoped he would choke on it.

From breakfast to dinner each family fed their guests the best meals that money could buy. The guests reeled from one house to the other, burping and chewing antacid tablets, carrying tales to add fuel to the fire by praising or criticising each meal. Preeti's father urged his prized halwai to add more pure ghee to his sweets while Manu's father ordered a magnificent five-tiered cake made with fresh cream and filled with out-of-season Alphonso mangoes. If one party served rabri loaded with pistachios the other retaliated with kulfi flavoured with saffron. The palak biryani at the sangeet ceremony at the girl's house was matched by a huge five kilogram tandoori fish baked with freshly ground coriander seeds at Manu's bachelor party. Since the boy and girl were not supposed to meet before the wedding, they only heard about the food served in each other's house from the guests, who were now beginning to look exhausted and pale and had to drag themselves with effort from one meal to the next.

"I'm sure my cholesterol level has increased in the last four days," said one aunt.

"I wanted to avoid that lunch at the boy's house, but when I saw that they were serving sharifa kulfi, I couldn't stay away," said another with a grimace as she swallowed a glass of Pudinhara for her dyspepsia.

Then came the grand finale—the wedding feast at the

girl's house. There was a shimmering air of expectancy as the guests took their places at a long table, which stretched into infinity like a railway line under the shamiana.

"No buffet-shuffet for me," Preeti's father had announced. "Only horses can eat standing up. I want a sit-down dinner for 200 people."

"My mother and grandmother did it. You women have no strength, or what?" he asked.

"We do not want to get our clothes all stained. You know I cannot even serve a cup of tea without spilling half of it. Anyway, I hate to see people eat like pigs, which they will, I'm sure, being from your kind of family. I hear they served only one kind of chicken at their dinner last night," said Preeti's mother.

So three dozen waiters were hired to serve the guests, but Preeti's mother agreed to supervise them. Like the leader of a band she marched up and down the long line of guests waving her hands. Since she could not keep up with the waiters, she often asked guests to have more when they had already been served. They nodded dumbly, unable to speak, their mouths full of food, and she moved on, trailing behind the nimble-footed waiters.

They ate like warriors who had returned from battle. They ate quietly, with stolid determination, till their stomachs were stretched as tight as the skin on a drum. Yet they took that one last helping. Then they leaned back, bloated and helpless against the wooden chairs, gasping for breath like fish out of water. They shook their heads in weak refusal as they were pressed to eat just a tiny morsel more. Some brave ones took another helping—"a very small one, just for formality's sake"— because they did not want to hurt their host's feelings.

Preeti's father stood at the end of the long table and watched them with a satisfied smile on his face. He rubbed his hands slowly and thought, "They will never forget this wedding till they die."

And the guests did remember the magnificent feast as they staggered out into the cool night air, flushed red and weary, avoiding the line of urchins who waited patiently for leftovers. But only till the next wedding arrived to erase it from their stomach's short memory.

Preeti never forgot. When she sat in the garden drinking tea, alone with her three divorced daughters, it always seemed to her that it had only happened yesterday. Although she could barely recall her late husband's face, the aroma of the rich food still clung to her senses. She often regaled them with tales about her grand wedding feast—a feast fit for the gods.

GREEN BIRYANI

400 gms basmati rice
1 kg mutton or lamb
8 tbsp oil
4 large sliced onions
4 green cardamoms
2 tsp finely chopped ginger
2 sticks cinnamon
4 cloves

1 bay leaf
½ cup thick yogurt
pinch of chilli powder
salt to taste
1 cup cooked and mashed spinach
1 cup stock

Heat oil and fry onions on low heat. Add cardamoms, cloves, cinnamon, bay leaf and then add mutton pieces. Sauté gently turning the meat over and then pour in the beaten yogurt. Add salt and chilli powder and keep frying the mixture. Then pour in the stock and cook on low fire till the meat is tender and almost cooked.

Now deal with the rice. In a separate pan, boil the rice till the grains are half cooked and then drain the water. Take another vessel, one with a heavy bottom, and put in half of the cooked meat curry. Then carefully top it with a layer of spinach and then spread the half-cooked rice and a dash of melted butter over it. Layer it once again with the remaining portions of meat curry and spinach. Top it with a layer of rice and melted butter. Cover the lid and seal it with a band of dough.

Cook on a slow fire and then open the lid just before serving. Savour the heavenly fragrance of spices and delight in the fresh green colour.

TIL ALU
(Potatoes with white sesame seeds)

250 gm small potatoes, boiled and peeled
1 cup white til seeds (sesame)
1 tsp turmeric powder
1 tbsp oil

2 red chillies

4 or 5 cloves of garlic

½ tsp fenugreek seeds

salt

Roast the til seeds gently till light golden brown. Grind to a paste along with the garlic and red chillies. Use a few drop of water but not much. You have to use a stone *sil batta* for the best results. Heat oil and fry the fenugreek seeds. Add the turmeric powder and then the til paste. Fry gently and then add the boiled potatoes. Mix well. Serve cold with rice. This hot spicy dish is from Nepal where it is usually eaten like a pickle.

MOONG DAL HALWA

1½ cups moong dal (split green gram)

1 cup sugar

½ cup milk

1 tsp cardamom seeds

sliced almonds and cashew nuts

Soak moong dal for 5 hours. Grind to a fine paste. Heat the ghee in a heavy vessel. Fry dal paste slowly till it changes colour. Add sugar, slowly mix it in. Boil milk with cardamoms. Add to the moong dal mixture. Keep frying on low fire till the milk evaporates and the fat separates. Add the nuts and serve hot.

Often served at weddings, this is a rich dessert, gleaming with ghee. A small helping goes a long way—usually to your waistline.

The Anger of Aubergines

◆

MRS KUMAR LIFTED THE curtains and looked out of the window. It was still early but sometimes he arrived at 12 o'clock when he had nothing else to do. He came and sat on the brown chair which he had bought at an auction at the American Embassy fifteen years ago.

Mrs Kumar remembered every little detail of their married life though they had been separated now for seven years. She did not find her estranged life any different from their dull, wedded one. The sullen mornings, empty afternoons and silent evenings had been replaced by a different kind of quiet loneliness which she found quite soothing, like the headache balm she often used. She had this small house to look after, the garden to grow vegetables in, the mango tree to guard. Her son wrote to her once a month from New Jersey and sent her a new sweater, of the same shade, every year. The unchanging pattern of the days was broken only by Mr Kumar's weekly visit, which took place every Sunday.

Mr Kumar was a brooding, taciturn man with no expression on his face except the occasional frown which sometimes appeared to show an intense, deep-felt agitation. Otherwise there were no lines on his bland features to mark the fleeting imprint of anger, love or hatred he had ever felt.

"I am what I am," he often said to anyone who cared to listen, and that was the truth. There was nothing more to him than the basic flesh, skin and bones, and one could see through him as if he perpetually carried an X-Ray film with him like a placard.

When he decided to separate from his wife, he did so with no emotional trauma or guilt. No reason was given and no explanation was demanded from either side. Though no papers were ever signed for a formal divorce, it was a clean, surgical cutting of ties which had never really existed. He had married her when she was 18 and he 28, because their families had long decided that they should be related through marriage so that their two businesses could merge. Mrs Kumar had brought a substantial dowry with her which had paid for his education in a prestigious university abroad, and also enabled him to buy his first suit, Rolex watch and car. They had produced one son whose conception shocked and amazed them both so much that no further attempt was made.

The son grew up in the warmth and confusion of the two joint families and did not recognise his father in the crowd of other men in the household. Till he was 18, he had been under the impression that his favourite uncle was his father. When he realised that Mr Kumar was the person who had brought him into this world, he was so stunned that he ran away from home. He was found a few days later, and before he could do anything drastic again, was married off by his grandfather to a suitable girl with a large dowry. Mrs Kumar had no say in the matter. Neither did Mr Kumar.

The day his father died Mr Kumar decided to live separately from his wife. The family, once so eager to see them united, were now indifferent since most of its members were either dead, senile or had emigrated to the U.S.A., where Mr Kumar's son had also fled when he came of age.

Mrs Kumar accepted the separation in the same calm, unruffled manner with which she had accepted her marriage to Mr Kumar, the subsequent taking over of her son, and her bleak married life.

Now only the Sundays remained to remind her that she had been married at all. She got up early on this day, bathed quickly and wore a fresh, starched saree. She finished her pooja faster than on other days and, hurriedly smearing a vermilion bindi on her forehead, went into the kitchen to marinate the meat.

The menu was more or less the same every Sunday because Mr Kumar had five or six favourite dishes which were rotated through the year. Though long separated from his wife whom he had never cared for, Mr Kumar had lunch with her regularly, once a week. The rest of the week he ate what his servant made for him, or went to his club. But come Sunday, Mr Kumar, like a murderer drawn irresistibly to the spot where he had killed his victim, headed home to lunch with his wife. He arrived at 12.30 sharp and did not have to knock or ring the bell because she always left the door open. He sat and read the newspaper while she added last minute touches to the food. Sometimes, he went into the room which had been their bedroom and checked the cupboards, but never touched anything. They never spoke to each other.

The aubergine bharta was ready and waiting to be garnished with fresh coriander leaves which she would fetch from her garden. This year she had managed to grow a bumper crop of vegetables and even the onions and garlic came from her back garden. She sliced the ginger into thin strips and dipped them in fresh lemon juice, because that is how Mr Kumar liked them. She had planted a lemon tree last year and now watched it carefully for signs of buds. Her plump, fair hands moved effortlessly as she chopped the onions, which she would then fry till they were crisp and dark brown and serve as a garnish for the pulao. Her eyes never watered when she cut onions—a virtue which had been a source of great amazement to her family.

"Let Sushma deal with the onions. She is really good at it," her sisters would say whenever they were cooking. Mrs Kumar felt very happy when she was called to cut the onions and rushed eagerly into the kitchen, tucking her saree purposefully around her waist. The others would make room for her in the crowded kitchen and sometimes even stand around watching her as she chopped and sliced with expertise. She became so good at her craft that she could even look up and still slice layers of onions as fine as paper.

Even now, sometimes, in the grey silence of the afternoons, she could hear her mother's voice echoing in the kitchen, "Let Sushma do the onions," and it gave her a surge of happiness.

Today she had made bharta, as well as dahi meat curry, because she had found two glossy, purple aubergines in the garden this morning. She had roasted them quickly on a wood fire in the back yard and then added tomatoes and finely chopped green chillies. She did not like to over-cook the bharta like most people did, for she felt it took away roasted flavour. The dahi meat she cooked on a slow fire till the gravy was totally absorbed in the meat, along with the flavour of cardamoms, aniseed and dry ginger. This was a Kashmiri meat curry called yakhni which she had learnt from her neighbour, but she liked adding a few touches of her own, like red chilli, to it. Sometimes after Mr Kumar left, she packed some leftover curry in a steel jar and took it across to her neighbour. She never rang the bell—just left it on her kitchen window so that she would not have to meet the husband who was a large, boisterous man with a wild look in his eyes which frightened Mrs Kumar.

She brought the bharta and placed it on the table next to the raita made with grated cucumber. Mr Kumar rustled his paper, shifted a little in his chair, but did not look up The pulao was steaming in the cooker and she began to spoon it out carefully onto a large serving plate, the last surviving relic of the English dinner set her mother had given her in her dowry. The pink and gold pattern of the china made the cashew nuts and raisins sparkle in their bed of golden brown rice and an aroma of cardamom filled the room. Mr. Kumar folded his newspaper and rose. This was his signal to come to the table. They sat opposite each other at the dining table, another find at the American Embassy auction. Mrs Kumar served her husband and then watched him eat.

"Is the salt all right?" she asked suddenly, in a low voice, startling her husband. He did not look up, just nodded, slightly unnerved by this sudden burst of chatter from his wife.

"Hope she is not going to start nattering away at meal times and ruin the food," he thought with a stab of irritation. She did not say anything more and after serving him another helping of meat curry, went to the kitchen to fetch the mango pickle she had made with fruits from the tree in her garden. Then she, too, sat down to eat.

There was no sound except for the occasional clink of a spoon touching the plate, Mrs Kumar's bangles jangling gently and Mr Kumar's satiated burping. He continued to eat, helping himself to more meat curry. He chewed methodically on the bones, his eyes shut in deep meditation. Then he piled his plate high with pulao, which his wife had just reheated, and added another large spoonful of curry. With deft fingers he mixed the two into neat balls and threw them into his mouth one by one. Under the table, his knees shook in joyful, contented rhythm. He ended the meal by ceremoniously lifting the huge bowl of raita and drinking the entire contents in one gulp. Before he left the table he ate a slice of mango pickle. There was no dessert because he had been told to cut down his sugar intake. His doctor had also told him to keep off rich, spicy food and he did—

all week. Abstention is what made this white meat curry, prepared with a fine blend of ginger and aniseed, as smooth as butter with an extra dash of red chillies burnt in pure ghee, so delicious. Yet it never failed to irritate Mr Kumar's stomach. And as he lay awake all night, tossing and turning in agony, chewing antacid tablets, he felt justified in leaving his wife.

YAKHNI (Dahi meat curry)

1½ kg mutton cubed, or lamb chops
4 tsp aniseed (saunf) powder
2 tsp saunth (dry ginger) powder
3 cups water
1 cup yogurt
2 tbsp mustard oil or any other cooking oil
red chillies to taste
salt to taste

Heat oil in a large saucepan. Add meat pieces along with water, salt, powdered aniseed and dry ginger. Cook on slow fire till meat is half cooked. Mix the yogurt with one cup of water and add to the meat. Simmer till meat is cooked. Before taking off the fire sprinkle crushed seeds of large cardamom. You can add a red chilli burnt in pure ghee if you want. Serve with plain boiled rice or pulao.

Train Fare

THE SEN FAMILY FORMED a separate little island on the crowded platform, though there were only four of them. They had spread their luggage all over and around the bench. Gopal Sen stood on one side, firmly, like a bookend, his short, portly frame protecting his aged mother and, at the same time, shielding his teenage daughter from any covert glances from 'bad types'. She sat, plump and pretty like a ripe fruit, on a large suitcase and kicked it methodically, although Gopal had warned her not to do so. His wife, Malati, stood in the middle of the group swaying like a palm tree in an oasis, tall and willowy, her saree pallav floating about her as she moved about in the dust-filled light of early morning, "Did you lock the garden gate?" her husband asked her once again.

"I cannot remember. Perhaps I did. Or else I forgot.

Shall we have some tea?" she asked, hoping to distract him, though she knew what his answer would be.

"Tea? Tea? Have you gone mad? Drink tea on a railway platform? From that tea-stall man? Have you seen his kettle? It hasn't been washed from the time of Queen Victoria. And his tea strainer? God! I feel sick just thinking of it. And so many men crowding around there," Gopal said, eyeing the crowd warily. "Did you tell the neighbours to look out for any suspicious people roaming around our house?" he asked for the fifth time.

Malati, feigning deafness, proceeded to check her handbag. As soon as she opened it her husband cried out, "Have you got the bedding slips? Did I give them to you or to Ma? Ma? Ma? Where is your bag? I can't see it. Thieves all around. Ma! Ma, wake up!" he shouted and shook the old lady, almost pushing her off the bench, but she continued to doze. "Is she dead or what? My god! Here of all places. . . with so much luggage. Ma? Ma? Answer me," his voice fell to a whisper and broke with fear.

Sita Sen opened her eyes slowly and fixed them with cold anger on her only son.

"I wish I had died, then at least you would leave me in peace. Caw. . . caw. . . caw. . . like a crow in my ears all the time. . . from the day you learnt to speak. The bedding slips are in your pocket. Now let me rest. You brought us here three hours before the train leaves. I could not even bathe properly," she said, her voice full of patient, long-suffering irritation. She sighed and shut her eyes once more.

"We are not the only ones. Look how crowded the platform is. It is good we came early. You don't know how these people push and shove when the train comes in. When travelling with women it is better to come earlier than later and be pushed around by strange men," Gopal said casting hostile eyes on the family standing next to them. There were no boys amongst them, he saw with relief, but there was one man who was below fifty. He could have evil intentions on Kajol or even Malati. He looked the type—dyed hair slicked back with oil and a checked handkerchief in his pocket. He wore blue socks. Gopal suddenly remembered his father's warning, "Never trust men who wear coloured socks or use aftershave or perfumes. They do it to attract women. . . other men's women, not their own."

Gopal returned to his earlier position. He did not want to leave the women alone for too long. This group of men looked very unsavoury.

"Let's move away from here," he said, scanning the crowded platform for a safer place for his women, shielding one eye with his hand as he stood on tip-toe, looking around anxiously like Noah surveying the land just before he began to build the Ark.

But Sita Sen refused to move and opened her paan box. She began to spread lime slowly on a betel leaf to show how firm she was about staying on her bench. Gopal then began a nervous pacing up and down the platform, looking for all the world like a restless tiger guarding his cubs.

While he was thus occupied, the rest of the family sat on the bench, people-watching and eating potato chips. Kajol eyed the boys in the group next to them and hoped they would be on the same train as her. She read a comic book hidden inside *A Tale of Two Cities*, a gift from her father for her last birthday, while her mother sipped a cup of tea she had bought from the tea-stall as soon as Gopal's back was turned. Sita Sen dozed and dreamt of the poori-alu she had eaten at this very station many years ago, as a young girl travelling with her family.

Their train arrived and much to Gopal's amazement, they all managed to get on board with no mishap. Just as Gopal sat down on his seat, counting his blessings, a loud authoritative voice broke the peace.

"These are our berths. Please vacate." A grey-haired woman sailed into view, cutting through the sea of luggage like a huge whale. Gopal tried to get up to defend his territory, but tripped as his legs got entangled in the straps of a bag.

"No they are not," he protested in a weak voice, trying to regain his composure as he stood with ankles bound, like a slave about to be auctioned. "It says here, '33, 34, 36, 37. . . Mr G. Sen and party.' You can read it," he added, reaching for the reservation slip in his shirt pocket. There was nothing there. All he could feel was the pounding of his heart. Black spots began to dance before his eyes. Had there been a mistake? He'd lost their tickets. They might be thrown out at some wayside station. He pictured his mother lying stretched out on a dark, desolate platform lit only by a lantern, his daughter screaming as dacoits carried her off into the night and his wife. . .

"Aren't you Joya from Lady Irwin, Simla?" his mother's voice interrupted his terrifying vision. The amazon, who was about to set her bags down to establish her rights, suddenly stopped.

"Is it Sita? My God! How old you look. I would have never recognised you but for the wart on your chin," she said, and with a flurry of saree pallavs and loud cries of delight, the two women pushed aside the luggage to embrace each other.

The train blew a plaintive whistle and reluctantly moved out of the station, squealing and whining like a newborn puppy. Sita Sen and her friend Joya sat down with a jolt and began to talk excitedly. Gopal watched helplessly as he tried to undo the bag straps around his ankles. Like mist before sunrise, the confusions and quarrels over seats vanished the minute the train began to move. Everyone, including many bitterly feuding parties, settled down amicably next to each other, chatting like old friends. Peace fell on the rattling compartments and though the train had not yet cleared the outskirts of the city, food packets began to be opened.

An aroma of pure ghee floated out as Sita laid out pooris on a huge steel plate together with a tiffin box of dry potato curry.

"Have some. It's made with whole coriander and ajwain seeds." She picked up a poori, wrapped it around some potatoes and offered it to her friend.

"No. . . no, too early. . ." said Joya in polite refusal, then quickly helped herself to the tempting poori roll.

"Some mango pickle? I made it myself," said Sita Sen, and Joya, disentangling her arm from the silken folds of her saree, reached forward eagerly once more.

"You were always good in Home Science, Sita. We all knew you would get married first. Is your husband still. . .

I mean are you. . .?" asked Joya in a soft, hushed voice, delicately balancing a piece of mango pickle in her hand.

"Gopal's father passed away seven years ago," said Sita. "Heart," she added, vigorously tapping her own generous bosom.

Joya chewed thoughtfully on her mango pickle and after maintaining a short respectful pause, she swallowed the pickle and said, "Mine went five years ago. Heart and kidneys. . . both," throwing a triumphant look at her old friend.

Gopal, who had been mentally preparing a polite speech to ask the lady to move her luggage, shifted nervously in his seat. He cleared his throat to speak but Joya looked straight at him and said, "Bit overweight, isn't he Sita?"

Gopal who was about to reach for another poori to comfort his nerves, stopped. His mother's friend fixed him with a cold look and said, "Heart is hereditary. Should be careful with fat."

"He was fat even as a baby. Weighed nine pounds at birth. Such fat, round cheeks he had. We called him Gulguloo," his mother said and everyone in the compartment, including those in the neighbouring one, looked at Gopal in awe. He heard Malati and Kajol giggle above him on the upper berths where they were perched like a pair of predatory birds.

He turned away from the tiffin box and stared moodily out of the window. He hated train journeys. Each time they returned from their annual pilgrimage to Hardwar the women started to behave oddly. The holy river Ganges, instead of cleansing them and making them more pious and well-behaved, seemed to have bathed them with a strange glow which made them laugh loudly, talk boldly to strangers and eat all kinds of disgusting food, like greedy beggar-women. His mother quickly took another poori, heaped a generous amount of potato curry on it and opening her mouth wide, took a big bite.

"Women should always eat in the kitchen after the men have eaten," his father used to say and now Gopal realised why. "How ugly they look chewing like cows, their teeth stained with food," he thought irritably.

The sound of contented mastication filled the crowded compartment as everyone ate in silence. Huge tiffin carriers balanced on the luggage, each one teetering at an angle like a row of leaning towers of Pisa. Curry spilled over the seats, shiny steel boxes tinkled and clanged and baskets were pulled out from under seats as people forced pooris, parathas, pakoras, vadas, cutlets, pulao, samosas and kachoris onto each other's plates.

Gopal hated sharing his food with strangers but his mother just ignored his warning look and called out to the people in the neighbouring compartment.

"Please have. . . ," she said, offering them a box of sweets. In that compartment there was a full scale feast going on with pulao, kebabs, and even halwa. Kajol looked down at them from her perch on the upper berth and hoped they would pass the food around. Her grandmother, it seemed, had read her mind and that is why she had made the offer of sweets to them. Now they would have to reciprocate, according to train etiquette, and offer them something. She was right. A young boy got up holding a bowl of sweet, red-gold halwa, passed it to her grandmother but kept his eyes on her. Kajol blushed and quickly looked at her father. But Gopal was busy frowning at her mother who was leaning down, her saree pallav floating. Before the boy could give Malati the bowl, Gopal had reached forward and snatched it from his hands.

Gopal looked around helplessly. His wife, having eaten six pooris and halwa from a stranger's kitchen, now lay curled up on the upper berth, humming softly as she read her book. There was picture of a couple kissing on the cover. Gopal glanced at his mother and hoped she would not notice. Worse still, what if some man passing by saw it and got ideas? Why couldn't Malati put a brown paper cover on these lurid romances she read all day long. He wished she would cover herself with a sheet. Anyone passing by could see her hips curving like a bow and the gleaming white soles of her naked feet. Kajol, he was happy to see, wore white cotton socks, though her skirt could have been longer.

The day passed slowly as the train travelled through dry, arid landscapes. There was not a single tree as far as the eye could see and groups of cattle huddled under rocks. Malati slept as though drugged and though Sita Sen tried to wake her up, she just muttered something incoherent and turned over.

"Good," thought Gopal. "Let her sleep on. She is safer there on the upper berth. If she comes down she might start chatting with the neighbours like she did at the Hardwar station tea-stall, recklessly giving her name and address to total strangers. What if they turned up one day looking for her?" Gopal suddenly saw a crowd of eager-eyed men with red socks and oiled hair standing in front of his house, banging wildly at the door as he tried to hide Malati. Overcome with terror, he shut his eyes.

People chatted, played cards and slept. Flies droned, swarming over the left-over food, children played noisily and stations flashed past with crowds of frozen passengers. Sita Sen and her friend, Joya, talked about old days, picking out forgotten threads from their memory, adding new touches wherever it suited them. Kajol, bored with her books, climbed down from the upper berth. When her father began to ask about her school work, she climbed up again, flashing a length of brown thigh which silenced the two boys chatting in the corridor. Gopal looked away, his eyes twitching with horror and shame.

The day wore on and the landscape began to change from brown to green. Soon it was twilight and the train ran straight into a line of flaming orange. Herds of cattle walked along the railway line and children shouted at them from the fields, waving bits of torn paper. As darkness began to descend outside, once more the food baskets were brought out. Now the bearer, too, joined in the clattering of plates as he brought huge trays laden with food for the passengers.

Malati woke up and asked for her dinner, still refusing to come down. "A difficult one, I see," whispered Joya and Sita just rolled her eyes.

They began to argue with the bearer who retaliated with spirit, much to their delight.

"Such cold food. What kind of gravy is this? Made

with dish-water I can see. . . You railway people just like to cheat us poor women."

The bearer laughed and shook his head. "You, poor? A rich noble lady of high class trying to fool me. . . a poor old peasant." The banter continued, each side enjoying the rally till Gopal could stand it no longer. He asked the man to leave, in a stern voice. The bearer ignored him and, grinning wolfishly, bowed to Sita, quickly casting an eye on Malati at the same time. Gopal reached into his pocket, gave him twenty rupees and the bearer, stunned into silence at this show of uncalled-for generosity, vanished at once.

As soon as dinner was over, most of the passengers started preparing to go to sleep. Sita's friend, Joya, was still chewing on a piece of chicken leg.

"Never eat chicken served on a train. It's never chicken, it's crow," Gopal's father had warned him and he happily repeated his late father's words loudly. Next door he could hear their neighbours packing up their tiffin carriers with a loud clanging of steel containers accompanied by equally loud burps. A few men walked past their compartment dressed in pajamas and rubber slippers. Gopal wondered how they could parade up and down in front of his mother, wife and other ladies dressed, or rather undressed, like that. One man even had his pajama cord dangling between his legs, much to Gopal's embarrassment. He was glad that Kajol was busy reading and his wife safely asleep once more. His mother and her friend continued to eat (now it was sweets from a box his mother had pulled out from her suitcase) and talk about old days in Simla. Over the sound of the rattling train he caught odd phrases. . . so erect. . . handsome and white. . . her breasts popped out. . . delicious chicken curry. . .

"What were they talking about?" Gopal wondered in alarm and when his distraught nerves could stand no more, he decided to switch off. It was safer to read his accounts journal and block all the sounds out than listen to this.

There were still twenty hours to go before they reached Panagarh, Gopal thought wearily. So many stations to pass with food stalls waiting to entice his mother. So far she had been content with eating the food they had packed from home but now that the tiffin carrier was empty, she would certainly look out for station food.

The train sped through vast, empty acres and now it was totally dark outside. Gopal accompanied his mother, wife, daughter and then his mother's friend, one by one to the toilet and waited outside the door, scowling like a fierce guard dog. Strange-looking men always gathered outside the toilets to play cards at night, and Gopal suspected that they were often drunk. Once the women were safely in bed, their curtains drawn, Gopal went to his berth next door and lay down fully dressed. His head throbbed with a dull ache. He regretted giving up his berth to his mother's friend but maybe it was safer for the ladies to be together, though he wished he could keep them in his field of vision. He hoped and prayed that they would not visit the toilet at night.

Moonlight streamed through the barred windows and fell on the sleeping figures at an angle, turning them into lifeless stone statues. The person above him snored gently and each time he turned Gopal watched the squeaking berth anxiously. They were made of strong steel, he knew, but how heavy was the man above him? He raised his head and looked out into the black night, and as the train shot through the darkness, he remembered travelling with his parents as a young boy.

His father would inspect the compartment for any stray beggars in hiding and would then park himself outside the compartment door and bravely defend his territory like a valiant soldier. His mother was always busy with food parcels, unpacking them the minute they sat down, ordering the servant to pour the tea even before the train had left the station. Sometimes, on long journeys, she brought a tiny stove along and cooked meals on the train. The servant would chop the vegetables and Gopal could still remember how his knife would waver as the train gathered speed and pieces of carrots and potatoes would roll off the plate into dark corners under the berths.

Once his mother made the servant get off at some small wayside station to buy more vegetables and then got into fierce bargaining with the vendor from her window seat. The train suddenly began to move and Gopal had never forgotten the servant's face, frozen with incredulous fear, as he watched the train speed past, leaving him on the empty platform. He was obviously found again because he returned to stay on at his parents' house, bossing Gopal all his life, till he finally died of old age. Gopal could not remember how his father managed to get him back but the feeling of utter helplessness he had felt as the train carried them forward and the servant's figure receded into a tiny, disappearing dot, still retained a fresh, nightmarish quality.

Lulled by the train's rocking movement, Gopal finally

fell asleep but then awoke with a start as he heard his mother coughing next door. Dawn was breaking outside and they were now passing through lush green fields of rice. Village women carrying brass pots walked through the fields and a row of bare-bottomed children sat along the railway lines, waving cheerfully at them.

"Kajol must not see them," Gopal's mind jumped with fear and he ran next door. The women were still safely asleep, their faces covered with their sarees. "How beautiful they look," thought Gopal as he stood near the door and watched them. "Like marble goddesses. . . so still and pure. Nobody could touch them and nothing could harm them if they just stayed frozen like this."

The train suddenly jolted to a halt and his wife opened her eyes.

"Can we have some tea? What station is it?" she asked, yawning. Her saree pallav had slipped from her shoulders and Gopal saw her breasts rise as she stretched her arms above her head.

"Go back to sleep," he said quickly, "I shall order some tea when the bearer comes by. Here, cover yourself with the sheet. You may catch a cold." He reached up to throw the sheet over her.

"Get tea from this station. I can see a chaiwallah," said Joya, "he has pakoras, too." She peered through the window.

"Which kind?" asked his mother sitting up quickly. Kajol was also beginning to stir.

"Cauliflower, spinach, onions and aubergines too, I think. . . He is frying them fresh."

Gopal pretended he had not heard and moved away

but behind his back he could hear his mother's loud voice calling out to the hawker. Soon a group of food vendors crowded outside their window. Crisp pakoras, hot jalebis, steaming tea in earthenware cups were thrust in through the bars and the women began to eat, greedily.

"Shouldn't you wash your face at least? Kajol, brush your teeth. Ma, what about your prayers, your blood pressure pill?" Gopal said, but they seemed to have gone deaf all of a sudden. Sita Sen held the leaf platters of food on her lap, passing them one by one to Malati, Kajol and her friend Joya.

"On a train you don't have to follow the same rules as you do at home. Anyway, God does not like me praying on a train. All this moving and shaking makes both him and me dizzy. And we might be passing through some low-caste village or, even worse, cremation ghats or burial grounds. Have a pakora, son. Will do you good. You know you always get constipated when you travel," she said holding up a greasy cauliflower pakora.

Gopal refused. He returned to his seat and began to gather his shaving things. There was already a queue for the bathroom and he wished the women had gone early in the morning, while it was still dark, like the other ladies on the train. Now these men would watch them as they came out of the bathroom, hair uncombed, top buttons on their blouses undone and faces wet.

"How dangerous life is when you leave the four walls of your home," he thought and sighed.

He waited for the bathroom to be free. Behind him he could hear men clearing their throats lustily and spitting out of the window. Finally, it was his turn and he quickly went in, as if escaping from a hostile crowd. The water gushed from the tap, cold and brownish, but he washed in it with joy. As he poured the cold water over his head he felt much calmer, and began to sing in a soft, broken voice.

He was surprised to find the women all clean and tidy when he got back. The sunlight, now flooding the compartment, seemed to have polished them and given them a new look. Malati had come down from the upper berth and sat knitting, her face washed and glowing, her hair tied back neatly, a red bindi on her forehead. Kajol was dressed properly in a long kurta with full sleeves, and his mother, too, had changed into a fresh, white saree and was reading a newspaper. Joya, the friend, was nowhere to be seen and Gopal did not ask about her in case she suddenly reappeared.

"Perhaps she got off at the station to buy more food and was left behind," thought Gopal, and felt much better. Why should he worry about unaccompanied women who travelled alone? He had enough worries about his own women.

But now everything seemed smoother, more under control. The women sat quietly, sweetly, sparkling clean. All was well now. They were going to get home safe and sound. They had not been kidnapped, raped, or molested. They had gone to the toilet and returned safely. His mother had not disappeared at some wayside station. His daughter had not been accosted by goondas, no strangers had spoken to Malati in the last twenty-one hours and the train was on time.

Gopal's heart was filled with joy as he looked out of

the window and saw the familiar fields of his home town approaching. Soon they would reach Panagarh station. His car, with curtains on all its four windows, and his faithful old driver would be waiting to take them home. They could go in and shut the door behind them. The journey over, he would have nothing to fear till next year when the women once again stepped out of his protective care.

AMCHUR ALU

250 gms potatoes
1 tsp chilli powder
1 tsp coriander powder
½ tsp turmeric powder
1 tbsp ghee or oil
salt to taste
1 tsp amchur
½ tsp caraway seeds

Boil the potatoes and cut them into small cubes. Heat the ghee or oil and lightly fry the caraway seeds and then the powdered spices. Throw in the potatoes, stir and add a cup of water. Simmer gently and serve hot with pooris.

Mushroom Madness

◆

RAIN DRIPPED FROM THE deodar branches and formed a pool near his feet. Nath moved further into the shade of the tree but the rain still caught him, drenching his back and head.

"I will catch rain fever and die. Then they can live together happily in my house, sleep in my bed," he thought, taking a long pull at his bidi and, as his heart filled with a rush of self pity, he suddenly felt much better. He looked up and saw that the sky was slowly clearing. Just a few grey-white clouds remained in one corner and he could see the rain moving beyond the mountain peak. A faint patch of pink sunlight now touched the tree-tops further up the hillside. Nath tucked his half-smoked bidi carefully behind his ears and began climbing up the path. The rain had made the stones slippery as glass and he had to walk slowly, taking shorter steps.

"I will reach home late today with nothing in my bag except for a few early plums. He must have gone to the other side of the forest and with his luck, would have found black mushrooms today," Nath said to himself with a sigh. "They will sit together in the kitchen. Chinta will fry the mushrooms in til oil and then she will eat them one at a time as he watches her." Nath could taste the slippery, spongy, fried black mushrooms in his mouth. He took out his bidi and lit it again. The tobacco mingled with the mushrooms as he exhaled clouds of smoke. He stood and watched the trail of smoke as it disappeared into the branches. He could make out the faint shape of Chinta's face in the cloud of smoke, just her eyes shaded by heavy eyebrows; and her nose. She followed him everywhere but always in fragments. Sometimes it was her face that peered at him from behind trees; sometimes her arms reached out to him, covered with her favourite green glass bangles. One day, when he was out ploughing, he met just her feet clad in the red plastic slippers he had bought her from the Renuka fair. They followed him for a while, flip-flopping in the wet mud and then disappeared. Nath wondered why Chinta tormented him, piecemeal, like this. He could have understood it if she was dead and her ghost was floating around divided into various parts. But Chinta was alive and living, in fact much more alive than anyone else he knew. She sang louder, walked faster, talked, laughed and ate more than any other woman in the village. Like a heavenly golden swan she shone amongst the drab she-sparrows at village gatherings.

Nath had met her at his aunt's funeral feast in her village which was at the other end of the valley. Chinta was 16 years old, plump and glowing with health like a pregnant cow. Her large, firm hips and her breasts promised many sons. Though she was ripe for marriage, Nath was amazed that no offers had yet been made for her.

"Her eyebrows join in the middle. It means she will always cause strife wherever she goes," a village elder told him, as Chinta walked past them carrying a plate loaded with besan ladoos. Nath's eyes followed her till she reached the end of the courtyard and then he saw her furtively crushing a laddoo in her mouth before she placed the plate on the floor. She turned around and saw Nath staring at her in amazement. Instead of looking ashamed at being caught red-handed, eating before the men had been served, Chinta giggled and, from far away, offered him a laddoo hidden in her soft palm, moist with sweat and sugar dust.

They were married as soon as the next auspicious day was available because Chinta's father was worried Nath might change his mind.

"Fortunately, his parents are both dead and his uncles can be silenced with a bottle, maybe two, of rice wine. But I'm afraid some interfering relative might break up the match. Then we will have this girl on our hands all our life. Let him feed her from now," he said to Chinta's mother when she objected to the unseemly haste.

Nath brought Chinta to his village which was a day's walk away along a narrow, tree-covered ridge leading to the other side of the hill. All along the way she sang in a loud, broken voice and laughed and skipped over rivulets, behaving like a carefree girl instead of walking quietly, at least five steps behind him like a new bride should.

"You will get lost if I let you walk ahead. I know this path better than you," she said when Nath tried to overtake her. The village women called out to Chinta. "Caught yourself a murga at last, eh? See you don't eat him up." Chinta laughed and turning towards them, spat out the seeds of blackberries she had been eating all along the way. When they stopped to drink water at a spring, she forced a handful of wild blackberries into his mouth, and the juice dripped down to mark a purple trail on his new wedding clothes.

He should have asserted himself on that very first day. Stood firm or given her a beating. Now all was lost. He was a slave to her demands. Both of them were her slaves, Nath and Mohan. The villagers laughed and jeered when they both tried to carry the grass she had cut, raced each other to fetch water for her, fought over ploughing her fields, giving her presents. Nath had given her all his land but Mohan had built a new house for her with carved pillars.

Though it was three years ago, Nath clearly remembered the first day Mohan had walked into the house asking for a bottle of lamp oil.

"You are Kanta mausi's nephew from Rajgarh, aren't you?" Nath had asked, giving him not only the oil, but a new box of matches and a bidi. How did he know then that he was allowing a serpent into his house? Worse than a serpent, because this man did not slither off as a snake would have done, after biting him.

Mohan now lived with them as Chinta's co-husband. He had to share her with him like the pradhan's wives in the village shared a husband. The women were used to it, in fact they even liked each other's company, but for a man it was torture. The joint eyebrows had brought strife just as the old man had predicted. Her breasts had fooled him with false promises—Chinta had still not given him a son. Maybe it was God's wisdom, else how would they know whose child it was? But he loved her more than ever, everything about her—her strange demands for food, her quick temper, her lazy ways had brought him joy till this man arrived and divided her in half.

Nath hardly spoke to Mohan now, but earlier they had fought every night when Chinta began to prepare for bed. Like cocks fighting in the village fair they had circled each other with clenched fists, and once Mohan had scratched his face with a wooden lice comb. But ever since the day she had picked up a burning log from the kitchen fire and chased them out of the house during one of the quarrels, they kept away from each other.

"She will tire of him, he is a simple-minded lout. They are not even married properly. He hasn't paid her father any bride money," Nath would reassure himself every night. As the first husband, he had the right to sleep in the same bed as Chinta but he often woke up and found her in Mohan's room which was a loft above the kitchen.

Tonight she would be there again because Mohan must have found the black mushrooms which she was so greedy for. Fresh green ferns, out-of-season vegetables, rare fruits from the plains, black mushrooms, rhododendron flowers, blackberries were some of her favourite foods. While the other women in the village were happy with dal and five thick chappatis with a lump of fresh white butter, Chinta would only eat these rare fruits. It was as if she were a forest goddess who had to be constantly placated with rare offerings otherwise her wrath would fall on them.

"If she was with child all this foolishness could be forgiven," an old woman in the village had said one day when she found Nath looking for blackberries in the forest. "But she is as barren as the rocks. Otherwise you think she wouldn't have produced a brood by now, with two men sharing her bed every night? Give her a good thrashing instead of berries, you fool!" she had screamed and had begun to pelt him with stones. Nath had dropped all the berries as he fled down the hill.

For the last one week Mohan had been luckier than him. He had found a secret source of black mushrooms in the forest which he kept bringing for her. If only he, too, could find something rare, something she had never tasted before, that would please her so much that she would come rushing into his arms at night.

Nath threw his bidi away and sighed. Folding his palms, he looked up at the sky as if expecting an immediate response from the gods. A golden-backed woodpecker flew across, screeching, settled on a deodar tree nearby and began to peck at the bark. As its drumming echoed across the forest, there was a sudden flurry of feathers and Nath saw a pheasant run out of the circle of ferns. He leapt forward and caught the bird in one quick swoop. Surprised at his own deftness he looked down at the pheasant in awe. He could feel the bird's heart beating under his palm. He let it go. The bird scampered away down the hillside with a faint chuckle. It was then that Nath saw the clutch of eggs lying under the ferns. Seven, glossy, ivory eggs lay in a circle on twigs and stones. Suddenly, Chinta's face loomed up before him, her arms came forward to touch him and her fingers danced on his cheeks. His heart was pounding as he bent down to pick up the eggs and he whispered grateful thanks to the forest gods who had answered his prayers. Nath remembered the last time he had found quail's eggs for her many years ago. Just two—but how happy she had been. She had taken them from his hands gently and broken one by softly hitting it on the grinding stone. Then, tilting her head back, she had swallowed the yellow yolk, raw. Taking some wet clay from the kitchen doorway she had smeared the other egg with it and placed it near the kitchen fire.

"The ashes will bake it and then in the morning, I will mix it with walnuts, jaggery and crushed gum. It will bring me a son," she said looking at him. The light from the kitchen fire lit up her face, danced on her neck and cheeks and Nath had known she would sleep in his bed that night.

The raindrops on the ferns wet his hands as he reached down to pick up the eggs. Nath placed all seven in his cap and put them inside his shirt. They felt warm against his chest and he remembered the pheasant's heartbeats on his palm. The bird was nowhere to be seen but he could hear a low chuckle far away. Nath took four eggs out from his cap and put them back in the nest. Holding the rest of them close to his chest, he began the long climb down. He took the longer cattle path this time because he was afraid the eggs would break.

"Let Mohan reach before me. I have found a treasure today. Nothing he brings will beat my find," Nath said to himself and laughed out loud.

Chinta's slippers were outside the kitchen door, the room was empty. She could not have gone into the fields because her dupatta, along with the scythe, was lying on the floor. Nath felt a cold fear pressing down on him, draining all his joy as he walked around the hut looking for her. She had run away with Mohan. He had always known that one day she would leave him. He had lived with that fear every night he heard her footsteps going towards Mohan's loft. Nath looked up at the loft with anger and hatred . . . then saw her lying on the floor.

"He has gone. He has gone!" she cried, beating her hands on the floor as if she wanted to break her bangles like a new widow. "I knew one day he would leave me, but so soon. . .What is there for him in Haripurdhar? Just rocks and snow! I will die. . ."she whispered, reaching her hands out blindly for him. Or was it for him?

She watched him indifferently as he took the eggs out from his cap and then turned her face to the wall, hicupping softly. In the evening, she calmed down a bit and ate the pheasant's eggs, not raw this time but boiled in salted water. After that, she ate whatever he brought for her but without joy or laughter, hunger or greed. Soon she began eating thick rotis like the other women and then she ate only rice gruel which she used to hate so much, and Nath knew her wound would never heal.

The hut was so silent now without him, the loft dark and crawling with black spiders as if none had ever slept there. Nath missed him. He needed his envy. Chinta's eyes were dull and muddy now that they looked only at him. She soon began to look like the other women in the village and then, as the days went by, even more faded and old, because, unlike them, she was barren. She spent all her time in the fields now and her skin became as rough as the bark on old trees. Nath could not touch her any more and she slept alone in the loft amongst the spiders.

Sometimes, when the moonlight crept into the room from under the doorway, Nath thought about Mohan. Haripurdhar was not far, just a two day walk from their village. Maybe they would go there this summer when the forest paths were dry and, on the way, collect black mushrooms for him.

MUSHROOM AND SPROUT BHAJI

1 cup mushrooms
1 cup chopped green onions with leaves
2 cups assorted sprouted lentils
2 tomatoes
1 tbsp oil
½ tsp cumin seeds

Heat oil and fry the cumin. Add chopped green onions but do not brown. Add the sprouts, tomatoes and mushrooms. Fry lightly and serve hot. This quick vegetable dish can be added to and stretched endlessly with a variety of other vegetables like grated carrots, cabbage, boiled potatoes and cottage cheese.

Constant Craving

◆

FROM HER BED, SUMITRA could see fragments of the sky. It was still dark and the moon, a thin half-circle, shone wickedly, like the edge of a newly-sharpened knife. The circle grew smaller as she watched. When she shut one eye, it twisted itself into a silver snake. She hated the moon, so shamelessly strutting across the sky, playing games with her and making her miserable. Her fast would end only when the half circle had changed into a full, glittering moon, but that seemed so far away that she could not even think about it. At the moment she just wanted the moon to leave the sky and let the daylight come through. Then she could have a cup of tea with milk and three teaspoons of sugar.

Sumitra had been a widow for only a year and though she kept all the fasts her mother-in-law had asked her to, she still felt furious pangs of hunger. Her stomach hurt and there was a strange metallic taste in her mouth. Monday fasts were not so bad because she could have fruit and milk. Tuesdays meant a little extra effort because Ma insisted they wake at 4.00 a.m to pray for their dead husbands. How Rammohanji would have hated their discordant chanting had he been alive. He had never woken up before 9 o'clock— all her married life she had had to tiptoe around the house, barefoot, till he awoke because her slippers made a faint tapping noise on the floor which disturbed his sleep.

"Maybe he still gets angry wherever he is. Maybe we are disturbing his eternal sleep," Sumitra thought as she looked up at the moon. "Please go. Let it be dawn. Then I can have tea," she whispered.

The moon remained fixed at the edge of the sky and Sumitra wearily shut her eyes.

"The moon, as it waxes and wanes, tells us when to fast. It protects the virtue of widows and keeps the souls of our dead husbands at peace, of course, only if they are in heaven," Ma had said a week after Sumitra's husband died. "The moon is our saviour, pray to him to give you the patience to be a widow. Fast, Sumitra, fast when the moon tells you. Your body should not be warm and plump, smelling of rich food, onions and garlic. You are not old like me as yet, otherwise it would have been easier, but try to be pale and thin as if the blood has drained from your veins." She showed Sumitra her frail, bloodless arms. "It is safer. . . no man will look at you," Ma added to Sumitra's amazement because she could not remember any man, including her late husband, Rammohanji, ever looking at her. But she fasted as the moon ordered and ate only fruit on Mondays and Tuesdays. Yet she still remained plump and her face glowed with a healthy, warm colour.

Sumitra drew the curtains and as she lay down, her stomach growled softly like a mildly irritated tiger.

"Only two more hours before I can have tea. In four hours, I can have a glass of milk and then after six hours, one piece of apple."

For Sumitra, this fast on the extra auspicious day of Ekadasi was the most difficult because it meant she could not even drink water for 24 whole hours. What she found bewildering was that, instead of getting used to the strict regime of fasting and eating less and less food, her body had turned defiant and decided to rebel. It craved foods she had never tasted even as a young girl. For the last one month, on Monday fasts she had dreamt of choley, paneer tikka, dahi kachori and even tandoori chicken—which she had never eaten in her life.

She shut her eyes and tried to pray.

"Make me your servant, oh Krishna! Make me your slave," she sang in a low, broken voice. Suddenly she remembered a jam sandwich she had once eaten many years ago as a child. The sticky, sweet taste filled her mouth and she felt the warm, melted butter and crimson jam on her lips. "Make me your slave. . ." she sang louder as her stomach gave a faint rumble of protest, then gradually settled into a mild ache. Yet the moon lingered on in the sky. "Go, you filthy creature, go. . ." she cursed and then immediately folded her palms and asked for forgiveness. "Make me your slave. . . make me your servant. . ." she cried, till she fell asleep.

She dreamt of choley once more. This time Rammohanji was eating them with her and urging her to take some more gravy. She woke up with a start. The moon had finally gone. Sparrows chattered near the window as she raced downstairs to the kitchen to get her cup of tea. Raghu, the servant boy, was still sleeping so she could have as much sugar as she wanted without Ma getting to know. The tea, milky and sweet, was so delicious that she felt dizzy for a moment. She shut her eyes and felt the warm liquid travel down her throat, caressing her softly.

"Sumitra, have you bathed yet?" Ma's voice was so shrill that it startled her.

"I thought I would have tea first. . . then. . ." she stammered, holding the cup firmly in her hands as if afraid Ma would take it away.

"You must bathe first and wash your hair before you break a fast. You know that, so why do I have to tell you each time. Go, go bathe quickly," Ma said and pointed to the door. "The fast will be wasted. No merit is gained unless rules are obeyed," she added and took a sip of tea, curling her lips back with distaste as she always did whenever she ate or drank anything. "Ashes and dust. . . ashes and dust is what I taste in my mouth," she would mutter, before finishing a plate of sweets with quiet determination. Yet she remained pale, thin and old, like a good widow should, Sumitra thought bitterly.

Choley with crushed samosa, that is what Rammohanji had given her in the dream. Sumitra had eaten them once by the roadside on her way back from school and had been punished by her father. He had locked her in the bathroom for two hours and when her mother protested, he had shouted, "Greedy girl! I will teach her a lesson she will never forget." And she had never forgotten the taste of the crisp samosas drenched with a thick, brown, choley gravy. In her dream the plate of choley was sprinkled with raw onions and Rammohanji was picking them out one by one and putting them into her mouth. The image, so vivid and yet unreal, unnerved her. Was her late husband trying to tell her something? They had never eaten together like this when he was alive.

"I think people change when they are dead. It is another world, after all. So many new faces," Sumitra thought as she filled a bucket of water for her bath. The tea had subdued her hunger pangs slightly but she felt strangely light-headed. She was 50 now, if she lived for another twenty years she would have to fast for maybe two thousand days, for two thousand waxing and waning moons and countless Mondays and Tuesdays.

"Maybe it would be better if I counted the days when she and I can eat and make a list now of all my future meals."

Suddenly an idea came rushing into her head and she was so shocked by it that she had to hold the tap for support. Water dripped over her face and ran down her breasts.

"I will have choley today. When everyone is asleep in the afternoon, I will ask Raghu to get me a plate of choley from the shop around the corner. I'm sure that is what Rammohanji was trying to tell me last night. He wants me to have choley. In fact, choley with samosa and maybe onions, too. He is telling me to have it. He is giving it to me with his own hands, a gift from him from heaven!" Laughing softly, she sang, "Make me your slave, Krishna. Make me your servant," as she poured water over herself.

The morning passed quickly as Sumitra helped her mother-in-law with her chores. They sorted out the linen, argued with the washerman, washed the prayer room, bathed and fed the idols and then ate their frugal meal of fruit and milk. All the while Sumitra thought of the plate of choley she would soon be holding in her hands. She dusted the huge, framed photograph of her late husband, hung a fresh garland of marigolds on it and lit a fragrant stick of jasmine.

"What a kind and generous man he was, and still is, judging from last night," she thought. She tried hard to remember some kind gesture he had made while he was alive. But all she could recall were his set phrases which he was so fond of saying to her each day, at regular intervals, throughout their married life. At breakfast it was, "Waste not, want not" as she passed him the toast. "Better late than never", accompanied his mid-morning tea and in the afternoon, just after lunch, it was "After lunch, rest a while, after dinner, walk a mile." This was repeated in the evening before they retired to bed, though Sumitra had never seen him ever take a walk even in the garden.

At last Ma went to her room and lay down. The house turned dark as the shutters were closed and everyone settled down for their afternoon slumber. In the kitchen Raghu slept near the door, clutching a cloth bag in his hands. Sumitra shook him gently.

"No! What. . ." he shouted as he woke up, startled, from his deep sleep.

"Shh! Keep quiet. Listen. I want you to go to the halwai's shop and get one plate of choley. . . choley with two samosas," Sumitra said quickly, not looking at the boy's bewildered face.

"But, you. . . Maaji. . . ." he stammered, rubbing his eyes.

Sumitra felt like slapping him but smiled instead and pressed a ten rupee note in his hands.

"Go quickly. You can have ice-cream with the change. Make sure the samosas and choley are fresh," she whispered. "Without onions," she was going to add but stopped. "Let Rammohanji decide. If there are onions on the plate then it is his wish," she thought, as Raghu gave her an odd look and went out into the hot afternoon sun.

The house was silent except for the tap dripping in the kitchen. Sumitra went out and sat on the verandah steps. As soon as Raghu returned she would take the plate and go up to her room. She would lock the door and sit on the bed. No, maybe she would sit on the chair near her husband's picture. It would please him to see her obeying his wishes. She would eat very slowly, nibbling at the hot green chilli which always came with the choley. She would savour the slightly sour and spicy grains of choley and then bite into the crisp pastry of the samosa, letting the potato filling melt slowly in her mouth. She would not swallow quickly but allow only tiny morsels to go down her throat, bit by bit, so that the delicious, hot, spicy, sour and salty flavour would linger.

The road beyond the gate was empty except for a pair of crows. They called in shrill, belligerent tones as if accusing Sumitra of succumbing to her greed. She quickly waved her arms to chase them away but they ignored her. Finally, Raghu's head appeared above the gate but his hands seemed empty. Sumitra felt her mouth go dry. As he came nearer she saw the blue plastic bag twisted around his wrist.

"Did you get it?" she asked eagerly, though she could smell the pungent aroma of hot choley. Raghu placed the plastic bag on the verandah steps and began to count out the change.

"It was only four rupees. The ice-cream was two. . . so here is. . ."

"How painfully slow this wretched boy is," Sumitra thought as she watched the precious plastic bag glow like a jewel in the afternoon sun. Just a few more minutes and then she could eat.

"Raghu!"

The voice shattered the peace of the quiet house and struck them like lightning. Sumitra froze as Raghu ran to take cover behind a pillar. Ma came out shading her eyes with her hand.

"What are you doing here? Did someone come at this odd hour?" she asked Sumitra in a irritated voice. Sumitra stared at the plastic bag which was now fluttering in the breeze like a victory banner.

"What is this rubbish? These crows must have brought it. Wretched birds of doom!" said Ma and kicked the bag with her foot. For a frail old lady she had a lot of strength, and it landed right near the crows. They tore open the bag at once and began to peck at the samosas greedily. Sumitra watched the brown choley gravy spill out to stain the road.

"Come, let's go in. The sun will make you ill," said Ma.

"Had the crows got any onions with the choley?" wondered Sumitra, as she slowly followed her mother-in-law into the house.

KHATTEY CHOLEY

1 cup kabuli channa

2 medium sized potatoes, halved

salt

1 tbsp oil

1 onion, sliced

1" ginger, sliced

1 tsp amchur

1 tsp cumin

1 tsp coriander seeds

2 cloves

1 small stick cinnamon

2 cardamoms

1 small whole, dried red chilli

fresh coriander

1 onion, chopped

It's always a good idea to soak the channas overnight—it makes the cooking process less laborious. Pressure-cook the channas with the potatoes and salt until tender. Remove potatoes. Break up one potato and slice the other. Heat the oil in a pan and fry onions and ginger until golden brown. Add the potatoes and fry some more. Dump the channas into this fried mixture, add the amchur powder and let the mixture simmer for a couple of minutes. Take off heat.

Dry roast the cumin, coriander seeds, red chilli, cloves, cinnamon and cardamoms until a delicious, spicy aroma fills the kitchen. Grind with a little water to make a paste and stir into the channa. Decorate with chopped fresh green coriander and chopped onions. Guaranteed, no leftovers.

Moonfish by Moonlight

◆

THE SOUND OF BREAKING glass awakened Soni. She covered her face and tried to go back to sleep. Then she suddenly remembered it was Friday and sat up at once. The entire household was already awake and when Soni went into the dining room, her mother was sitting at the table, shouting at the servants.

"Idiots, can't you do anything right? Do I have to do everything around here? Why am I feeding you louts mounds of rice, gallons of tea? Am I running a dharmshala here?" she screamed. Her voice rose in an arc and raced through the open doorway into the kitchen. But the servants carried on with their work, ignoring her and chatting amongst themselves in low voices. Her voice hit their indifferent backs and bounced back at her like a boomerang. Bhatu, the cook, who had known her since she was a young girl, waited till she had finished her early morning tirade, placed a cup of tea in front of her and returned to the kitchen. Soni's mother took a sip of tea curling her little finger delicately.

"How bitter this tea is," she muttered, somewhat calmer now. "So the princess is awake at last. Have you forgotten what day it is?" she asked in a mildly belligerent tone as soon as Soni sat down at the table.

Ever since Soni could remember her mother always spoke in this querulous fashion. In fact they had got so used to her "Am *I* to blame?", "Should I do *everything*?", "How *can* I?", "Do you all think. . .?" all through the day, that when she did ask a genuine question once in a while, no-one answered her, and the onslaught of hurt and offended queries began again.

But today Soni could see that her mother was genuinely agitated. She put her arms around her. "Don't worry, I haven't forgotten, mama. How *can* I?" she asked, sounding to herself very much like her mother.

The Great Moonlight Picnic. They had planned it for so long, arguing, rearranging, cancelling, postponing and, finally, tonight it was going to happen. The guest list had been a long battle between her parents. A meticulous selection was made by weighing each invitee's present relationship with the family and carefully examining their past behaviour for any misdeeds. Ten fortunate people, who did not know they had won after such a bitter struggle, were finally chosen. Mr and Mrs Shukla and their two daughters, Mr Nath and his new bride, and Mr and Mrs Pant had happily accepted the invitation. Two aunts and one doctor cousin were added to the list at the last minute by her father who said, "It is good to have a doctor. After all, you never know. . . and the aunts can take the left-overs home."

There had been no difficulty in choosing the picnic site, because in their town their was only one likely place. The Maroda lake. This large expanse of muddy water was surrounded by a park where, during the day, hundreds of morning walkers strolled, children played cricket and young couples courted under the shady trees. Soni wondered what it would be like at night. She was excited and slightly afraid. Ramvati, who was sixteen, only two years older than her, often went there at night. "To catch moonfish," she said, but Bhatu always laughed as if it were not true. Soni could not believe her parents were taking her to something so rare and unusual like a moonlight picnic where anything could happen.

"I do not want anything to happen. So I have ordered an extra car to follow us. The food can go in there," said Soni's father before he left for his office. Her mother waited for him to leave the room and then flopped down on his chair, the most comfortable one in the room.

"So much to do. This picnic will kill me. Does anyone care?" she asked, looked up at the ceiling and soon her gentle snores filled the room.

In the kitchen, Bhatu put the pieces of chicken which he had already smeared with yogurt into the fridge and began kneading the dough.

"Throw in some more flour. Let us have a picnic feast, too. She will never know how much we are eating in the dark," said his nephew who was new to the household and thus not expected to be loyal. Ramvati, the maid, giggled but quickly stopped as Bhatu looked at her sternly. She pulled the grinding stone out from under the table and piled the onions on it in a small heap. Squatting comfortably on the floor, glass bangles clinking, she began grinding the onions, slowly adding pieces of ginger. Bhatu and his nephew watched her as she moved her strong, plump arms to and fro over the stones.

Bhatu had decided the menu much in advance, and though Soni's mother had fought and argued with him for days, had not budged an inch.

"Sahib said it is all right," he said each time she tried to change the menu. The chicken biryani would be ready by the afternoon. It would remain in the copper vessel, sealed with a rope of wheat dough which would be broken off just before serving. Dahi fish he would start making as soon as Ramvati finished grinding the masala for it, and the paneer he would prepare last of all so that it remained soft. He would make sukha zeera alu for Soni and an aubergine dish with yogurt that her mother liked and that would be enough for all, including the servants. They would carry a stove with them and make the parathas and pooris when they reached the Maroda lake. He did not have to make anything sweet because Sahib wanted an English pudding which would come from a shop.

"Waste of money. Full of rotten eggs and flour," Soni's mother had said, but only to him when they were alone in the kitchen.

The food was ready by the evening despite Soni's

mother's gloomy voice predicting disaster at every step. Finally, Soni took her away from the kitchen and forced her to lie quietly in her room as she rubbed Tiger Balm on her forehead. Bhatu quickly packed the food in two giant tiffin carriers before she could come down, and by the time Sahib arrived everything was standing in an orderly line near the door. The tall tiffin carriers gleamed like brass soldiers, the tava sat firmly in the basket along with other pots and pans, the stove was tied up in a bundle along with the kettle, and the dough packed into one huge steel tin.

Ramvati, dressed in her best saree, hair plaited and tied up with a pink ribbon, held the jar of ghee in her lap as if it was a precious baby. The nephew, a bit awed and subdued by now with the preparations, stood quietly behind this impressive line-up of picnic luggage. Bhatu had packed some nimki, chidwa and salted peanuts in case some people got hungry before he could serve the meal. Soni's mother had asked her to pack the rugs, two packs of cards, three torches, a dozen candles, six small towels, one bedsheet, four large bamboo fans, a bundle of newspapers and a big bottle of Dettol. At the last minute she had thrown in an antique silver dagger "for our protection. . . just in case". It lay on top of the massive bundle, its coral and turquoise stones winking in the evening light.

It was dark by the time they set out, after many false starts. Soni's father had forgotten his antacid pills and Bhatu suddenly panicked and jumped out of the car to run to the kitchen for one last look. The guests sat waiting in their respective cars, each armed with their own bits of luggage. The convoy moved slowly through the empty, dimly-lit streets and, as the pots and pans rattled under her feet, Soni felt like a refugee fleeing a war-torn city.

The headlights lit up the narrow path shaded by babul trees. Maroda tank—so cheerful, dull and safe in the mornings, now loomed ahead like a dark mystery, a vast sea of trembling shadows and dancing fireflies. Their voices sounded so loud that everyone began to whisper as they got out of the car. Suddenly Ramvati shouted.

"Look, Soni didi, there is a full moon!" she cried and ran towards the lake, her saree floating out behind her like a sail. Soni wanted to follow her, but was afraid and stood still.

"Bhatu, get the soda and ice out," her father ordered in an unusually shrill voice and everyone began talking at once. They spread the rugs out close to the cars and the men sat down to play cards at once. The women stood uncertainly for a while, watching them, and then when Bhatu got the stove out, they quickly gathered around him like moths.

"Shall we start getting the food ready?" asked Soni's mother and for once in her life, got an immediate reply.

"Yes!" they all shouted in unison.

The women laughed as they bumped into each other trying to carry the huge tiffin carriers. Soon they lifted their sarees higher and tucked them in at their waists. Their ankles, always hidden, flashed in the moonlight as they ran about like happy children. Bhatu sat in the middle of this bustle, hovering over the stove, and began heating the ghee to fry the parathas.

"We'll roll out the parathas. Bhatu, move aside. Go,

see the lake. We will be the cooks tonight," Mrs. Nath declared in an excited voice which carried far into the night, and made the men look up from their cards and smile.

Soni sat with the other girls and listened to them talk about a recent film they had seen. She could see Ramvati far away near the edge of the water. Bhatu's nephew was with her. Their bodies seemed to float, touch and move apart slowly. Soni suddenly felt breathless with fear. The fragrance of spices floated in the air, mingled with the musty smell of wet earth, and somewhere near them an owl hooted urgently.

"Ramvati," Soni heard her voice echo as she ran towards the lake. "Ramvati, come back. You'll drown!" she cried. The nephew quickly turned around and then laughed, his eyes glittering in the moonlight.

"I will save her," he announced, and stroked Ramvati's arm slowly as if tracing a pattern with his fingertips. Soni heard Ramvati say something to him in a low voice and they moved away into the shadows.

The women had begun to serve the food though the men were still playing cards.

"Come on. Are we going to wait for you all night?" cried Soni's mother. The doctor threw his cards down and shouted, "Let us not keep the gentle ladies waiting all night," and then winked at the men. Everyone laughed, including her mother whose face was glistening with sweat. She looked so strange in the moonlight, like someone whose face was familiar to Soni but whom she had never met in real life, never spoken to.

Soni ate a spoonful of rice and then pushed her plate away. She could hear Mr. Shukla gnawing on a huge chicken leg like a hungry ferret, smacking his lips after each bite. Her father's hand loomed out of the shadows to pick up a plate of fish.

"Good! Good! Good!" he muttered, his mouth mis-shapen and swollen with food. Mrs. Nath stood behind him, giggling as she kept pouring more gravy onto his plate. He caught hold of her hand. "Stop! You'll kill me!" he cried and as they laughed and wrestled playfully, the rug was splattered with drops of red-brown gravy.

"Soni, Soni, eat, beta," her mother called out from a dark corner. She reached out to Soni, her hand clutching a fistful of food. "Come, sweet girl, mummy's pet. Have one *girai* from my hands. Just to make me happy. Come my poppet," she lisped, making kissing noises with her lips.

Soni turned her face away as the smell of food began to make her sick. What was happening to everyone? Was this moonlight madness? She looked up at the sky and tried to remember the names of the stars her father had once pointed out to her. As she watched, a meteor streaked across the sky and fell on the black lake.

Ramvati came out of the shadows. She ran towards them. Her wet saree clung to her legs and was covered with streaks of mud. She was holding something in her hands. "Look, baby, a moonfish. I caught a pretty little moonfish for you!" she cried in a strange, high voice. Then she came and stood above them, laughing in the moonlight, the dead fish gleaming in her hands. The pink ribbons were no longer on her plait and her blouse was pushed off her shoulders.

The men stopped eating and stared at her. The women looked down and muttered in soft angry voices.

Soni wanted to throw herself on Ramvati, hide the shining, wet curve of her breast. She wanted to scream at her for standing there, so shamelessly beautiful. Scream at her father for staring at her wet skin. She wanted to snatch the moonfish from her hands and throw it back into the lake. But she could not move. They all sat still, frozen in the silvery moonlight, their eyes on Ramvati's offering.

DOI MAACH (Fish with yogurt)

1 kg fish (Rahu or Surmai)

1 tsp sugar

1 cup yogurt

1 tsp salt

1 cinnamon stick

2 large cardamoms

4 cloves

1 tbsp oil

2 tbsp ghee

A few sultanas

1 tbsp grated ginger

1 green chilli, deseeded and sliced

Cut fish into medium-sized pieces and marinate in yogurt for one hour.

Heat oil and ghee together in a saucepan. Add cinnamon stick, cardamom, cloves, sultanas. Fry lightly for 2–3 minutes. Take fish out of the yogurt and carefully place, one by one, in the saucepan. Pour the rest of the yogurt over the fish. Add salt and sugar and simmer for 20 minutes or till fish is cooked. Take care not to stir the mixture; instead, just shake the pan lightly, like James Bond's martini. The fish pieces should stay firm and not crumble while serving. Add ginger and chilli. Serve on a flat dish. Should be eaten with steaming hot, plain boiled rice.

Food to Die For

◆

MY GRANDMOTHER FRETTED OVER everything. But a few weeks before grandfather's shradh she would go into a major flap. Her two favourite worries were cleaning the house and cooking a special meal for the occasion. The third source of anxiety—finding a priest to feed—she kept in reserve so that she could give it her full, undivided, frenzied attention. The house, already as clean as a well kept hospital ward, was now filled with the heady aroma of phenyl.

"Did you get the 'lamp black' one?" she would ask Gopal the servant boy, suspiciously, about a particular brand of phenyl, as she could not read English. Then, holding the bottle under her nose, she would take a sniff as if it were vintage brandy. The room where my grandfather's annual shradh ceremony was to take place was swabbed and swept till bits of cement began to come off the ancient mosaic floor and were collected by the servant as concrete proof of his tireless effort. Each day I thought that Gopal, a young boy of fifteen, would protest and throw down his duster and broom. But he did not. Instead, he became even more frantic as the days went by, sweeping and cleaning like a man possessed. He crashed into furniture and tripped over tables as he swept the floor with his phenyl-drenched cloth, snarling at anyone who came in the way of his octopus-like crawl across the floor. No one was allowed into the shradh room except my grandmother and him. In the afternoons, when the rest of the house was asleep, I would see my grandmother sitting with Gopal on the floor in a corner of that vast room. Whispering like two conspirators, they searched for any hidden trails of dust. They were hysterical one day when they found that a sparrow had flown in while Gopal was not on guard and had left three tell-tale blobs on the floor.

"Maybe it is a good omen," said Gopal, trying to avoid blame.

The cleaning phase finally ended. Then began the food phase. The main items on the menu, kheer, poori and potato curry remained fixed, but two new dishes had to be planned. The whole family debated this issue.

"Make gobhi. Dadaji liked it," said my brother with a selfish desire for cauliflower.

"No he did not, it gave him wind," said my grandmother.

"Let us have carrot and peas then," my father said.

"Carrots ! Are my relatives rabbits that I should feed them carrots? And what will the priest think? We will make phulmakhani and paneer curry," she said decisively and the subject was closed.

Gopal and my grandmother had already begun preparing the ingredients for each dish. Almonds and raisins had been washed till they lay pale and wan on the plates, huge quantities of best quality basmati rice had been scanned for hidden stones, and potatoes had been selected with the same sharp-eyed scrutiny as she had chosen brides for her sons. With only one day left for the shradh, the kitchen was now reserved for their exclusive use. Some eager relatives had already begun to arrive. As soon as the women stepped into the house, they plunged right in, without being asked, to help with the preparations. They took off their slippers, washed their hands and sat down on the kitchen floor. Within minutes they were working in perfect coordination with my grandmother, yet I never heard her give them any instructions. Though they worked quietly, once in a while someone would offer a tid-bit of interesting news for the group.

"Meera bhabi has had another girl," and a collective sigh would go up. "Ramlalji's house was sold for one crore," would bring a gasp of amazement. Some remarks were perennial favourites and repeated every year. "Bibiji, your eyes can pick out even the tiniest of stones from the rice," a cousin would say and my grandmother would lob back her set answer, "We ate pure ghee and in our youth there was no TV to make our eyes water."

Another regular one, a favourite with the old lady was, "Maaji, how do you keep the house so clean?"

"This boy helps but I have to watch out for any. . . ."

she would say arching her eyebrows and throwing a swift glance in Gopal's direction and all the women and Gopal himself, understood the silent accusation.

This was the right time to start searching for the priest. Each woman gave her report about new priests they had seen at various weddings, funerals, shradhs, naming ceremonies and house-warming pujas. The height, weight and age, along with any other qualifying features, of each priest were related and my grandmother listened with rapt attention, her faded eyes gleaming like old silver. She rejected them all, one by one, and leaning against the kitchen wall began to cry, "What will happen to his soul? How will I show my face in heaven when we meet? Oh! Help me God, help to me to find the right one," she sobbed while the women looked on with awe, their hands still busy peeling and chopping.

Last year's shradh was ruined for my grandmother because the priest would not eat anything at all. He pushed the kheer away because his blood sugar was high, and ate only two pooris because his doctor had told him to avoid fat.

"Who has ever heard of a priest on a diet? What is the world coming to? Next they will ask for salad. How will they help me cross the river of death, when my time comes, if they eat only boiled food?" Grandmother cried for days while we greedily lapped up the leftovers, including the priest's lion share.

Though the high point of the ceremony for my grandmother was feeding the priest, which would grant her many plus points in the scheme of heavenly merit, for the last ten years she had not found a man worthy of her culinary skills.

Some were too bedraggled, and she suspected they were not genuine brahmins because they had cracked, muddy feet.

"A real priest has feet as smooth and clean as a baby's since they are washed regularly," she said. Others she rejected because they had a shifty look in their eyes which did not seem learned or high-born enough. One fellow who came to her door, smelling of cigarettes, was scolded and sent away in spite of having the advantage of bringing along his own cow for the shradh. Some were too fat for her liking, others too emaciated and sickly. One, to her horror, spoke in English and drove a car, while another did not know his Sanskrit well enough. Every year one member of the family was chosen by my grandmother to find the priest, and one by one we all failed her. This year her glance fell on me though I had been hiding from her eagle eyes.

"You know how to drive, you can go to the temples on the outskirts of the city and search. Remember to check that he doesn't have a blood sugar problem," she ordered.

So I set off with a heavy heart, like a distraught prince who has been ordered by his bride's father to cross seven rivers, confront the giant and bring back the lost jewel. At every temple I had to wait in a queue to meet the priest and when I finally reached the window where the audience was being given, he had already been taken.

"You understand, sister, how difficult it is for us to make everyone happy. We can eat only once a day. There are five of us here and we have been booked till the end of next month."

I searched all day but could not find anyone to fit my grandmother's specifications. The ones that were available did not have the right weight, level of cleanliness and other-worldliness. One priest rejected our offer outright when he heard the menu—"too rich"; and another, the offerings—"too little"; while a third agreed, but suddenly changed his mind and accepted the next, higher bid. Finally, when I was about to accept defeat and return home, an old priest took pity on me and brought out, from nowhere, a scrawny looking boy.

"Take him, he is my son; but let me warn you, he is still a learner."

The fledgeling priest was all wrong, from his unkempt hair to Nike clad feet, but my weary heart accepted him in all humility.

I returned home in the evening to find cauldrons steaming and all the women chopping vegetables in a frenzy.

"Did you find him?" they asked eagerly. I nodded evasively and went out of the kitchen.

"What is he like?" my grandmother asked.

"He is young," I replied truthfully.

"That is good. He will eat well and fearlessly. Maybe I should make one more vegetable. Gobhi will be good since he is young and will not worry about wind." She turned away happily and called out to Gopal to buy five kilos of cauliflower. I was surprised that she did not ask for any more details. Her faith in my choice made me feel terribly ashamed about whom I had selected, and all night I lay awake afraid of what the next day would bring.

It was still dark when I heard my grandmother and Gopal in the kitchen. Gradually, as dawn began to break the other women joined them. They worked silently in the dim light as if performing a secret ritual, their movements slow and precise and their silhouettes shifting and merging like ghosts dancing. The kheer bubbled and burped in a huge brass cauldron as Gopal stirred it continuously, the steam rising to cover his face with a fine mist. Two women sat on the floor with a flat plate of flour—while one kneaded the dough the other kept pouring small amounts of water. They did not speak to each other but just nodded together every time the water was poured as if taking part in a pantomime. The vegetables which had already been chopped earlier were now thrown one by one into the kadai, along with spices, and the hot oil quickly changed their colours from pale green and white to deep red-browns. The final menu was potatoes in a rich, red gravy made only with tomatoes (no onions or garlic), cauliflower with just a dash of ginger to highlight its flavour, phulmakhani and paneer coated in a mild gravy, yogurt with a sprinkling of crisply fried bundi, and, of course, the mandatory kheer which was now going to simmer on a low fire till it turned a special shade of pink. Only Gopal was allowed to stir the kheer because his arm movements were the best coordinated, being used to hard labour.

"You young women have no strength in your waxed arms," my grandmother would say if smooth-armed women tried to touch the kheer. They were happy to be let off because a slight hesitation in the stirring process would make the milk sulk and fall in a heavy layer at the bottom of the vessel or, worse still, taint the kheer with a faint odour of burnt milk which only my grandmother's sharp nose could pick up at once.

I could not bear to watch them preparing this feast for a trainee priest who, I was sure, had no desire to follow in his father's profession. But when I went to fetch him later that morning he was ready and dressed for the part. A saffron shawl was draped elegantly around his frail shoulders making him look older, and his long hair, now worn in smooth, well-oiled curls, added that extra touch of priestliness so desired by my grandmother. His feet, I noticed, were now bare. We sat silently for a while because I did not know how to address him. 'Sadhuji' would be presumptuous because he had not yet qualified for the job, and 'beta' might be too familiar and probably even blasphemous.

"I have never sat in a Maruti car before," he said suddenly leaning forward eagerly. His eyes shone with joy and he looked like a schoolboy dressed up for a play. He told me he was studying in an English medium school and hoped to go to college. "I have learnt enough Sanskrit to be able to recite the various mantras so that I can carry on my father's work. You see, madam, we get free housing quarters at the temple," he explained fiddling with the music system in the car.

When we reached home, I got out of the car, walking ahead of him so that the impact of his small height and under age status would be slightly diffused.

"What is this?— a baby priestling!" cried my brother. "Better get some milk ready, or maybe Farex," he added, laughing. My young priest heard him but carried on walking up the stairs, his head held high. His eyes took on a cold, steely look which his ancestors must have used to put many a cheeky prince in his proper place. He greeted my grandmother with folded hands but gazed far beyond her shoulders as if already seeing her in the context of the next world. Throughout the shradh ceremony, which he conducted with dignity and skill, he did not once smile. Not when my father tripped over the brass pot as he tried to wash his feet; not when my brother asked him to 'fast forward' the prayers; not even when his dhoti got caught in the new umbrella which was being offered to him. He glanced at all the gifts he would receive at the end of the ceremony with a cool indifference which impressed even my cynical brothers. He just nodded briefly at the collection which consisted of seven brass utensils, a folding bed which my grandmother had bought instead of the charpoy to keep up with the times, three crisp white dhotis, an expensive shawl, a huge black umbrella, a flashy red torch in place of the obligatory lamp, and a massive pile of bedding to last him a lifetime.

Then he sat down to eat. At first he ate slowly, chewing each mouthful thoughtfully. The women watched from the kitchen door, and my grandmother hovered above him like a genie freshly emerged out of the brass lamp which glowed near the mat upon which he sat. She did not take her eyes off him as he ate, anticipating his needs before he could make even a slight gesture. No words were spoken. Slowly the vegetables vanished, pooris disappeared without a trace, yet his plate was never empty, like Krishna's mythical bowl. The women rolled out pooris faster and faster and Gopal fried them frantically. The boy priest kept eating at a slow but unwavering pace. My grandmother beamed. The women took turns to come out and gaze upon him with wonder. Gopal applauded his 25th poori with the same gleeful cry he kept for test match victories. Finally, when we, the unbelievers, were getting a bit tense about there being nothing left for us to eat, he stopped with a gentle burp, but not before he had drunk a cauldron of kheer by holding it up to his mouth and finishing it in one breath. My grandmother wept tears of joy.

"You come every year, panditji," she whispered.

"Your food is the best I have eaten. Next time, can I bring a few friends? They are not priests, but..." he hesitated, shedding his earlier haughty stance now that the ceremony was over.

"You bring anyone you want. I will feed you and your friends on this day, as long as I live."

A year later, my grandmother passed away. The young priest came one last time to pray for her soul and to eat his last meal in our house.

"The food is not the same without her," he said, but ate non-stop with his usual gusto, to ensure that her journey across the river of death to greater heights was smooth and easy. The shradh ceremony is no longer held by our family and a token amount is given to charity instead. But I know that the boy-priest, who must be middle-aged by now, is still eating his way through life, like a caterpillar, with the benevolent spirit of my grandmother watching over him.

PHULMAKHANI (Lotus Seeds) AND PANEER

250 gms phulmakhani
250 gms tomatoes
250 gms cottage cheese (paneer)
½ tsp coriander powder
½ tsp cumin powder
½ tsp turmeric powder
salt to taste
half a cup plain yogurt
1 tbsp oil

Heat oil in a kadai till it is smoking hot. Fry the coriander, cumin and turmeric. Add chopped tomatoes and keep stirring till the oil separates and the mixture is deep red. Put cubes of fresh panir and half a cup of yogurt, diluted in just enough water to cover the panir. Add salt and simmer for a few minutes and then add the phulmakhani. Serve at once while the lotus seeds are crisp and fluffy.

Dead Man's Feast

◆

WINTER WAS ALMOST OVER in Neri and the first buds of almond blossom had begun to sprout on the hillsides. The pradhan lay dying on his bed. He had been dying for a month now and everyone in the village, busy planting the new crop, had forgotten about him.

The day he had been struck down by lightning in the forest, the people of Neri had gathered around his bedside all day, watching him in hushed awe.

"Curse of the wives!" they had whispered. But when he showed no signs of giving up his soul, in a frenzy of spasms and blood-curdling screams like the old woman in the neighbouring village had recently done, they lost interest and began to fade away. Only the family remained by his bedside now, arguing and planning his funeral in loud voices which echoed like drum-beats inside his head.

He had had so many children from his five wives that he lost count after the first four. Some had died in infancy, some had run away to the city, but even so, quite a few remained to torment him on his deathbed. Fortunately, the daughters had left sooner, taking their numerous noisy children with them and he no longer had to feed their brood.

His three, or was it four, sons who worked in the town nearby, were still here but he was hoping they too would leave soon, because now they had begun to grumble about 'leave without pay'. They sighed impatiently as they sat drinking tea by his bedside.

"Nowadays it is so difficult to get even one day off from work. Our new sahib allows only two deaths per person in a year—one for mother and one for father," said his eldest son who had a good government job.

"What about a dead wife?" asked one of his younger sons who had just got married.

"So far no one has applied for leave on such account. We will have to wait and see when the situation arises," answered the older one in a serious, judge-like tone. They all kept quiet for a while pondering over this future dilemma.

"Do wives ever die?" thought the pradhan. He had married five times and each one of them was as strong, healthy and alive as ever and kept appearing every night in his dreams to abuse him. Thank god none of them was with him any longer, They had all moved away from the village and lived god knows where.

None of the wives had come to see him and he was not sure whether he was happy or hurt by their absence.

"It is better they don't come. Let them remember me as the lion I was and not this shrivelled-up stick. Maybe some of them have died, that is why they are not here. But Mani would have told me. She knows each one of them better than I ever did." Pradhan tried to call out to Mani but his sons' voices, so loud and jarring, drowned his feeble call and he lay back, silent and angry. "Why don't they go away and leave me alone to die in peace? Where is Mani?"

Mani sat outside in the courtyard and cleaned the rice. A flock of pigeons formed a circle around her and gleaned the rice husks from the stone floor. The mild spring sunlight warmed her face and soothed the ache in her bones. She would make khichdi today for the pradhan for he could swallow a little more easily now. He missed eating good food now that his teeth had gone. Mani wondered if the sons would leave today by the four o'clock bus, then she would have to cook only for the pradhan and herself. The daughters had gone last week, promising to come again soon, along with his sisters who lived in the villages near by. Mani knew they would only come for the funeral now, but she said nothing. She was thankful to god that his wives had stayed away though the villagers were angry about it.

"Five wives, bought with good bride money, and who is sitting by his death-bed? Only one old woman who is not even his mistress," they muttered and sent baskets of corn, vegetables and rice to her.

Mani was not old when she came to live with the pradhan after her only relative, her brother, had left the village to work in the city, taking his family with him. He had asked her to go with them but she knew his wife was not too keen.

"We have looked after her ever since your mother died. But now she will be a burden in the city," she had heard her sister-in-law say one night when she was in the kitchen, washing the dishes. Mani had stayed back, promising to look after their small bit of land for them.

"Good you did not go with them. Why should you live in a matchbox in the city? They would have made you their servant. Better to stay here. You can come and cook for me," the pradhan had said to her one day when they were gathering the corn in his fields. "No salary, but food, and a roof above your head," he had added with a worried frown as if already regretting his reckless generosity.

Sixteen years had passed. They lived quite happily together in his spacious, old house which was one of the largest in the village. She could hide herself in one of the many rooms when the pradhan brought girls to the house or when his men friends came to play cards.

"Of all the women in the world, you had to choose the ugliest one for your old age!" she had heard one of his friends say, when he had come across her accidentally in the courtyard. Pradhan had just laughed. He never got married again, and though she waited each night, watching the door with fear and hope, the pradhan never called her to his bed, either.

"We are planning to go back today," said the elder son not looking at her. Mani covered the rice basket and stood up.

"Shall I make some food for your journey?"

Without waiting for an answer she went into the

kitchen. She was so happy that she wanted to sing as she kneaded the dough for the pooris. Then feeling guilty, she added a generous amount of ghee to the dough and began to gently slap out perfect circles on her palms.

"Mani, Mani. Have they gone at last? Promise me you will not call them again, not even for the funeral feast. Have they not already eaten all the grain they can for the last, I don't know how many days," he cried and Mani had to wipe his face with her dupatta. She put a little khichdi in his mouth with her fingers and waited for him to swallow. "Do you remember which one died?" he asked after she had finished feeding him and given him a small bit of tobacco to chew.

"Nirmala," said Mani, pressing his feet. "But no-one is certain whether she is dead or has become a sadhuni. Hari says he saw her in the Churdhar caves last year when they had taken the devta on his winter journey."

"How rough your hands are, Mani, like pieces of old bark. Nirmala must be dead. She could never become a sadhuni. She was too fond of drinking rice wine. Her hands were as soft as a baby lamb's stomach," the pradhan said. "Why did she leave me?" he asked turning his face away from Mani.

"Because you brought Uma home and they fought all day, they even broke the red glasses with painted flowers you had bought for Rs 125 from the Chinaman. One night you threw them both out and locked the door. They slept in the cattle shed. The cows gave no milk that morning. They left the village soon after that and then you met Geeta at the fair and married her," Mani replied, her hands rubbing the soles of his feet.

"Was Uma really the second one?" he wondered. "No, can't be. There was another woman, not Uma, after Nirmala. She had a black mole on her breast." He shut his eyes and tried to remember her face but his mind was a sheet of black. All that he could prise from his hazy memory were soft, slippery bodies without any faces. Only Mani's face loomed before him, ugly and gentle. He quickly opened his eyes. "There was one called Shanti. Which one was she?" he asked, trying to raise his head.

"The fifth and last one, after Draupadi. Do you want to eat some kheer? There is plenty of milk now that everyone has gone," Mani said.

"No! No!" cried the pradhan in an irritated voice. "Shanti was the third one, the one who made such good rice wine. Smooth, but went down your throat like fire. Nirmala was the one who drank and Shanti was the one who made the wine. What a pity she had to die. I wouldn't mind some wine now. Are you sure Nirmala is dead and not Draupadi? She was the sickly one. Always complaining of some illness or the other whenever I called her to my bed," he muttered and began to cough. The small room echoed with his rasping coughs and Mani tried to rub his back. Slowly he became quieter and lay down, resting his head on her lap. She could feel his heart beating against her palm and she remembered the goat she had once held just before it was to be slaughtered at the temple.

"Just rest now. I will get some wine for you later from the neighbours," said Mani and began to rub his forehead, making circles with her fingertips.

He shut his eyes and suddenly they appeared one by

one, all his wives, and began circling his bed like vultures.
They laughed and tried to touch his face with their fluttering hands.

"Come and see me die. Come you bitches, come to my
bed!" he cried and Mani held his head tighter in her lap.

"Nirmala, Uma, Geeta, Draupadi and Shanti. That was
the order of your wives." Mani said, her voice low and soothing as if she was singing him a lullaby. "Go to sleep now.
They have all gone. You are tired. They have made you tired,
these wives," she whispered.

Nirmala, Uma, Geeta, Draupadi and Shanti. How well
she remembered each woman. Nirmala was the most beautiful, with large eyes and brown gold hair. She had often
walked past Mani's hut, laughing and talking in a shrill voice,
always heavy with child.

"Does he ever leave me alone? Get another wife I say
to him. You are too much for one woman," she used to say
when they were at the well, her voice soft and content.
Mani had heard her screams a few days later when the
pradhan brought Uma from the neighbouring village.

"I will tear her eyes out! She is a witch. See how long
her fingers are. She will kill him. I know, I know. . ." Nirmala
had cried and run to every home, pleading with them to
send Uma away from the village. The elders listened and
nodded their heads, while their wives made sweet, strong
tea for her.

"What harm is there in taking a second wife?" they
said. "After all the pradhan is a wealthy man. He has to
spend his money somehow. He already owns much of the
land here, has 18 cows and six buffaloes. He bought a gold

watch last year which told the date as well as the time, so what else can he buy now except for another wife?" So saying they asked Nirmala to have some more sweet tea and go home to the pradhan.

Soon Nirmala began drinking rice wine every evening. She would sit in the courtyard and abuse Uma who was now pregnant.

"Die. . . you whore! Die on your childbed. Bleed to death!" she screamed, her voice slurring more and more as the evening passed. Soon her face became puffy and lined like stale dough, and her fine eyes no longer sparkled like they used to when she talked to her friends at the well. She slept out in the courtyard and smelt so rotten that even her two sons refused to come near her.

One day when Mani was cutting grass in the pradhan's fields she found Nirmala lying on the path. Her shirt was torn and her dupatta covered with mud and wine stains. Mani went to fetch the pradhan but she took care to call him out alone.

"What a nuisance this woman is. What fine hair she had, like silk, and now look at her. Worse than a barren cow. Get rid of her, Mani. Give her to someone. They do not have to pay any money for her," he said, lighting a cigarette with a lighter he had bought recently from the city.

"It works with petrol. That is what they put in the car to make it run," he explained to her and they both watched the blue flame suddenly light up like magic.

Behind them Nirmala moaned and tried to lift her head but she soon fell back and Mani covered her face with her dupatta so that the flies would not bother her. Her brown gold hair gleamed as it lay spread out on the ground.

The pradhan sighed. He wished Nirmala had not left when Uma came. They could have stayed together and looked after him, sharing their duties like other wives.

"Why did Uma leave?" he asked. "Mani, Mani, why did Uma leave? Was she the one who died?" he whispered as if Uma's ghost lurked near.

"Do not talk so much. Why don't you go to sleep? Shall I rub some sweet almond oil on your forehead?" asked Mani. Her hands ached and she could not keep her eyes open. The lamp was burning very low now and she moved the pradhan's head from her lap and got up to pour some more oil into the bottle. Her shadow looked frightening on the walls as it broke into two separate halves.

"Mani, do not go. It is not morning yet. Why did Uma leave? She was happy with me. I gave her a gold chain. Rs 450 it cost me. She was so lovely. She could make the best black dal in the village. Thick and rich like butter. But Nirmala made better kheer. Geeta could make the best meat curry and Shanti made the best rice wine. Maybe she was a good cook, too, but she was with me for such a short time that I cannot remember what she was good at, except that she knew how to press a man's legs till all the tiredness vanished. Only Draupadi was no good. I'm sure she is the one who died, useless woman. No good in bed and no good in the kitchen. But she had pretty green eyes," he muttered and began to cough again.

Mani woke up with a start. She did not know when she had fallen asleep. The pradhan was tossing about, mumbling in a broken voice, his face covered with sweat. Mani fetched a wet cloth and wiped his face and arms.

"Oh Mani, my ugly one, bring them," he cried and pushed her hands away. "Draupadi. . .come to me. Uma, Uma, Nirmala. . .come to me!" As he called, his body shook with a fit of violent coughing.

Pretty, plump Uma had run away with the pradhan's cousin who had come to stay with them from the city. Mani had seen them together in the early morning bus but didn't tell anyone about it. Who would ask her anyway? Surprisingly, Nirmala, too, left soon after, though her hated rival had gone. She took her two sons and went to live with her uncle who was a widower. Sometimes Mani met her, when she took the goats to the higher meadows beyond their village hillsides. Nirmala's hair was grey now but she still looked beautiful when she laughed.

"How is the old goat? Has he died of a disease as yet, or not? Tell him his sons are waiting for his money," she said to Mani, her lovely eyes flashing with hate. Her breath reeked of rice wine. Was she a sadhuni now or a spirit wandering about in the mountains? Mani wondered. Uma, she never saw again, but Geeta came to the village with her daughters because her sister lived there. Yet she never once came near her old house.

"I curse that house," she shouted, and spat on the ground. "The old devil can rot there with his new whore of a wife. Green-eyed witch!" She turned her beautiful face towards the house so that Draupadi could hear her.

But her curse was wasted because Mani knew that Draupadi, with the almond-shaped green eyes, was already the old wife and Shanti, a pretty young girl with big hips, was now sharing the pradhan's bed. He had told her when she had gone to collect money for the grass cutting.

"Mani, you are a good woman though god has made you as ugly as an old witch. But I never knew that a beautiful face can hide such venom. That green-eyed Draupadi bit my hand when I told her to heat some milk for Shanti. Shanti is not strong enough to work as yet after childbirth. Twin sons she has given me—like Sita. Luv and Kush I will call them."

And like Sita, Shanti too left her home and the village with her sons but no-one, not even the pradhan, could explain why. She had seemed happy enough, always singing away softly as she worked on the new sewing machine the pradhan had got for her, the only one in the village.

"I gave her two tolas of gold and never beat her except once, when she forgot to light my hookah. I even got that idiot brother of hers a government job. Women are so ungrateful—worse than snakes," he said when Mani gave him the news that Shanti had opened a tailoring shop in town.

"Thank god you are so ugly, Mani, at least you will never make a man unhappy," he had said before leaving for a long pilgrimage to the remote mountaintop temple of Churdhar.

Mani shook herself awake. The pradhan lay quietly now but she could see his lips moving in his sleep.

"Nirmala, Uma, Geeta, Draupadi, Shanti," he cried in a soft voice, again and again like a hungry man begging for food.

Mani heard a cock crow outside in the courtyard. The

sky was turning lighter and she could see the jagged line of the mountains emerge slowly out of the darkness.

"I will make kheer for him. Hot kheer with crushed almonds like Nirmala used to make. I will make black dal, too, richer than Uma ever made; and the pradhan will never have tasted meat curry like the one I will cook. Tender, soft pieces of goat's meat in a rich, green, spinach gravy."

Mani got up quietly, taking care not to awaken the pradhan, and went towards the kitchen.

"I will grind the ginger finely and roast the garlic in cow's ghee. If I soak the black dal now, it will soon be soft and ready to cook. The kheer I can put on a slow fire, after I have milked the cows. Everything will be ready by noon. Then I will bathe him, dress him in a new kurta and feed him slowly, one small mouthful at a time. The meat will be so soft that he will be able to swallow it easily. All day long I will feed him like a new-born sparrow. Kheer. . . meat. . . black dal. . . kheer. . . until he dies. Then his wives can come and take him away."

CHUNKY SAAG MEAT

1 kg mutton cut into cubes

1 tsp turmeric powder

4 onions, grated

3 cloves of garlic

2 tsp grated ginger

2 whole cardamoms

1 stick cinnamon

6 tbsp yogurt

1 tsp salt

4 tbsp oil

1 tbsp ghee

2 cup of lightly cooked spinach, mashed

2 large tomatoes, chopped

Heat oil and ghee in a heavy pan. Fry the ginger garlic, cardamom, turmeric and cinnamon. Add the meat, yogurt and salt. Fry till the meat is light brown. Add the tomatoes, one cup water and the mashed spinach and cook on slow fire till the meat is tender. This spinach meat curry has a thick green gravy which goes very well with plain rice or bread. For some reason Saag Meat always tastes better the day after it has been cooked, so I always save some and eat it the next day.

KALI DAL

1 cup black urad dal
4 cups water
1" of ginger cut into strips
2 large tomatoes, quartered
3 chillies cut into long strips
salt to taste
2 tbsp cream

This type of dal takes a while to cook. If you have the advantage of foresight, soak overnight to soften the grains. Then pressure-cook with water and ginger until dal is done. If it is a last minute decision to add this to a menu don't panic. Pressure-cook with the 4 cups of water. Wait for it to cool. Add ginger strips and pressure-cook again. The dal must now be soft and mushy. If it looks too dry, add some boiling water to the mixture. Drop tomatoes, chillies and salt into the pan. Keep stirring and mashing the dal until whole grains are not visible and the mixture is thick. As a final piece of extravagance add the cream and stir in. Take off heat.

This dal is absolutely delicious eaten with parathas or even plain chapatis.

Sweet Nothings

◆

THE CHOCOLATE SAUCE, warm and dark, dripped all over her face but she could not taste it. She opened her mouth wide, stretched out her tongue and tried to lick it off her lips but all she could taste was Pond's lemon cold cream. Reshma spluttered, began to cough and awoke to find herself alone. Ajay had already left for work and his clothes lay scattered on the floor. A damp towel lay near her feet on the bed. The bedroom swirled with the musky fragrance of his powerful aftershave, lemon fresh deodorant, anti-fungal foot powder and minty cool breath freshener.

Reshma picked up the hand mirror that lay on her bedside table.

"He's going to see that bitch today," she said aloud to her reflection, and as her voice echoed in the empty bedroom she noticed that her hair needed touching up. She would get red-gold streaks this time, but not too light other-wise people would think she was trying to look like that other woman. How awkward, and awful, that her name was also Reshma. Of all the women available in this city, and there were so many willing to sleep with her husband, he had to choose one with the same name as hers. Maybe it made it easier for him. Now he could safely call out Reshma . . . Reshma . . . in the throes of passion and both Reshmas would think he meant it for them, or perhaps not know whom he meant it for. It was so confusing and an added humilia-tion, as if that woman had stolen a bit of her, too, along with her husband. It was not as if Reshma was a common name, like Gita or Madhu. Her mother had named her after the famous movie star whose eyes, were green-gold, just like hers.

Reshma peered at the mirror and was once again soothed by the reflection of her two sparkling green eyes. She lifted her face and, stretching out her neck, began to pat her chin slowly with the back of her hand. Her soft skin, pale and transparent like old ivory, curled and dimpled beneath her hands and she felt her flesh quiver like jelly. Should she have a liposuction or whatever they called it?

Reshma studied her face as she tried to recall the strange dream she had had last night. Some dim images floated in her head about Ajay growing fat and round like a gas balloon, but they soon faded away and only a strong memory of chocolate sauce being poured on her, remained.

"I wish I hadn't eaten that cake last night, 800 calories in one second. Now, today, I will have to subtract that from the 1500 calories allowed. That leaves me with only. . ." Reshma reached for the slim book titled *Complete Calorie*

Counter lying on her bedside table. She looked at the cover picture of a blonde girl in a white swimsuit, holding a glass of orange juice in one hand and lettuce leaves in the other. A huge bowl of salad stood in the background while the lettuce leaves fanned the girl's face as if she were in a tropical forest. Reshma opened the book with a sigh and began to read. A frown gathered on her forehead.

"One pound of excess weight is 3,500 calories," the book stressed once more. "Therefore, if you are 11 pounds overweight, you have consumed 11 x 3,500 calories more than your body needs." Reshma looked away guiltily and shut the book. She already knew the chapters by heart since she read the book all day long, carrying it around with her in her handbag. She was beginning to hate the girl on the cover as much as the other Reshma, because both of them somehow seemed to merge into the same smug, slim, taut body which she could never have. Reshma put the book back on the table and looked up at the mirror again. The frown was still on her forehead, running across in fine crooked lines, and she quickly erased them by opening her eyes wide and forcing herself to yawn. She held the yawning smile for a few seconds and then slowly lifted her face, stretching her neck muscles till they hurt. She continued with her face exercises for a while, smiling like a crazed clown, squeezing her eyes shut, turning her neck from side to side, puffing out her cheeks and then got up and rang the bell above her bed.

"She is awake. I better go," said Amah and got up slowly. Raha the cook looked at her and shrugged.

"What's the hurry? She will do those jumps now. Up and down, up and down, above our heads. Wait till she finishes, then go. Have your tea. There. . . you can hear her now." Amah and Raha, holding mugs of tea in their hands, raised their heads and stared at the ceiling nervously as if expecting the roof to cave in. A loud thumping beat ran through the house, making the ceiling light sway.

"One day she will come down through the roof, I tell you," said Amah.

"I know. That is why I never sit under that hanging light. Come here near the door, we are safer here," said Raha. Amah picked up her cup and went to sit down next to him.

"You should see her doing the face exercises. Gave me such a fright the first time I saw her. I thought she was having an epileptic fit and ran to put a spoon between her teeth. She laughed and told me that these funny faces she made every morning kept her young-looking," said Amah. Raha clicked his tongue twice to show his disapproval and amazement at the same time. The noise was getting softer now and only a gentle thudding could be heard on the ceiling. They noisily slurped their tea, keeping a wary eye on the wildly swaying light.

"Why do you take so long to hear the bell!" asked Reshma petulantly. Amah did not reply and began to pick up the clothes strewn on the floor. It was going to be a difficult day.

"Sahib's gone to see that skinny one today. All that scent. Must be Wednesday then," thought Amah, who could not read or write. "I must wash the napkins today," she muttered and moved towards the bathroom.

"Leave my juice here. . . near the bed. Tell Raha to give me only fruit today. No breakfast. Wait. . . he can send up one slice of toast, but no butter. You make sure, Amah, that the toast is absolutely dry. And get me a banana too. No. . . no. . . Amah. Just wait," Reshma said and quickly picked up the diet book from her bedside table. "B. . . B. . . where is Banana? O.K. Here it is—Banana, big. . . 80 calories, medium. . . 70, small. . . 60. That is for English bananas. Ours are such skinny ones. . . must be only 60 calories, even less. Don't you think, Amah? Or shall I have a boiled egg? That is also 60 calories," Reshma chewed her lip and put her hand to her forehead. She quickly erased the frown lines that were about to gather. It was so difficult to keep a straight face all the time, but the book said each facial expression meant one more wrinkle. She sipped her orange juice slowly, putting her lips carefully against the rim of the glass and made her face blank.

Amah rested her back against the door as she folded the clothes. This perfume that Sahib used on Wednesdays when he went to see the skinny one always made her feel slightly dizzy. Her father also used to put this kind of attar on before he went out to play cards with his friends. One day she had stolen a bit of the oily perfume and, hiding behind the grove of banana trees near their hut, she had taken a drop and stroked it on her arms. Her mother found out at once when she came back to the hut and had picked up a broom to beat her.

"Smelling like a whore! What are you. . . a bitch on heat? You want boys to chase after you, sniff you?" she had screamed, thrashing the broom on her back. When her father died one day in the middle of a card game, Amah had run to the shelf and picked up the bottle while the hut was crowded with mourners. Her mother, lying on the floor beating her chest, had seen her, but had not said a word. Amah still had the attar bottle with her, wrapped in an old silk blouse Memsahib had given her. She often took it out to sniff the faded, musty scent.

"Get my bottle of hand lotion . . Amah?. . . where are you? That pink one. . . there. . . next to the powder. . ." said Reshma from behind the bathroom door. Amah handed her the lotion, catching a brief glimpse of her plump breasts, white and lined with fine blue-green veins like two unripe watermelons.

"Why doesn't Sahib like her?" Amah wondered as she began making the bed. Memsahib looked exactly like the goddess on the calender she had seen in Raha's room in the servant's quarters. Tall, plump, with flaming red-gold hair which cascaded down to her ample bottom in thick, snake-like curls. Sometimes in the mornings she did not look very pretty, but then Sahib always went out running at that time and never saw her like that, puffy-eyed, with a strange white mask on her face like an annointed cadaver. She looked totally different when she went out with Sahib in the evenings, dressed in silken clothes and jewels like a princess, her cheeks glowing pink, her lips blood red.

"If only she didn't have green eyes," thought Amah, looking at Reshma standing in front of the mirror in her dressing gown, "she would have been more lucky." Her mother used to say women with green eyes are the devil's creatures and men with green eyes, the devil himself. In their village there was only one girl with eyes like Memsahib, and she had drowned in the well during Holi. People said the full moon had driven her mad. The skinny one Sahib liked so much had black eyes and walnut-brown skin. Amah had often seen her with Sahib in the car on Wednesdays when she went to the market.

"Amah, do you think I have lost weight? See . . . here . . . a little bit around the hips. Can you see, Amah?" Reshma asked twisting her neck to look down her back. Amah looked away and continued to fold the sheets on the bed as Reshma scrutinised herself from all sides in the long mirror.

"Why do you try to become thin all the time? So healthy you are. Mother of two handsome sons. You should be fat and happy like a queen." Amah muttered as she smoothed the bedcover with her hands.

It was her two boys and one miscarriage that had made Reshma so fat. After each pregnancy she had to starve herself to get back to her former size. And each time the inches held on tight, gripping her body like a python that would never let go. Now, at forty-four, the fat had set into her flesh like cement. However much she tried, the layers remained embedded. She starved, living only on juices for weeks till black spots danced before her eyes. She exercised for an hour each morning, sweating like a pig, heart pounding till she felt it would burst out of her lycra leotard. She tried jogging but her breasts bounced up and down so much that they began to ache. Ajay did not want her to go jogging with him, in any case.

"You are just fine, my roly-poly, fatty baby. I like a bit

of flesh. It's nice to have something soft to hold," he said and patted her bottom. But she knew that the other Reshma was as thin as a boy. That woman had no breasts or hips at all, and Reshma had once seen her rib cage outlined against her skin as she danced with Ajay, clinging to him like an emaciated baby monkey.

"It's only sex. Don't fret, it will give you wrinkles," her friend Mimi advised. "Feel sad if you want to though I don't see any reason why you should cry over that creep, but keep your face blank. No man is worth a new set of crow's feet," she added. Reshma tried to sob with a straight face as they jostled side by side on their treadmills.

They met at the gym every alternate morning, and drank coffee with sugar substitute afterwards. Mimi was not thin but she was a heartbreaking two kilos less than Reshma, and her buttocks were firm, like a football player's.

"The only time I feel really happy is when I am on the treadmill. I don't care who Rajan sleeps with. All I want is to lose two inches more around my waist. Then I can die a completely happy and fulfilled woman," Mimi always said breathlessly as they did their sit-ups. Reshma tried hard to keep up with her but her heart began to beat so fast after the first ten sit-ups that she felt that she would have a heart attack on the gym floor. She could see herself lying on the striped mat, eyes staring at the ceiling, while Mimi and the other women carried on with their exercises.

"Would Ajay marry that skinny bitch? No, probably not. He would prefer to play the field, free at last of a fat, ugly wife," she thought and as tears welled up in her eyes, she began to do the sit-ups once more, slowly counting backwards, swallowing her tears and trying to keep her face wrinkle-free.

On her way home Reshma saw that the shops had put out stalls of firecrackers on the pavements.

"It's Diwali next week. I wish the boys could come home from boarding school. Then we could have a big family party with firecrackers and dancing. Like the old days." Ajay did not like playing cards so they never went anywhere during Diwali, except to wish his parents. Reshma suddenly felt a sharp pang of hunger as she passed the mithai shops whose brightly coloured sweets spilled out on to the pavements.

Saliva poured into her mouth as she remembered the taste of each and every sweet on display. There were shiny, gulab jamuns—120 calories each—which just disappeared as soon as you popped them in your mouth. Reshma preferred the thick-skinned, black, kalajamun which you could chew for a while, savouring the crunchy, dark, outer layer. Then there were tiny orange laddoos—250 calories—made with fine grains of sweet bundi, which she loved to eat after meals. Imrati, an orange swirl of delight—200 calories. Dreamy rasmalai floating in saffron milk—300 calories. Reshma gulped and took a deep breath as advised by her diet book.

To resist temptation, take a deep breath and remember the weight loss goals you have set for yourself. The desire to eat will subside.

As a child Reshma's father would take her to the mithai shops and allow her to pick out all the sweets she wanted.

She would stand on tiptoe and peer into the glass case which was filled with a sparkling range of white, pink, orange, green and golden-yellow mithai. There was burfi made with cashew nuts and pistachios, pale orange laddoos, slim, golden brown malpua floating in syrup, delicate and feathery balushahi, rubbery, sweet karachi halwa, heart-shaped dil bahar, delicate, golden patisa, sugar-coated channa murki, tiny, white, dripping with sweetness rasbhari and solid, chewy kalakand. She would point her finger to each one and the shopkeeper, hands sticky with sugar syrup, would throw them all into a large cardboard box. When the box was full he would weigh it carefully, adding an extra burfi or two, and then wrap it in shiny red and gold paper. The shopkeeper, who knew her father well, would lean down from the counter and offer her some sweets to taste, but Reshma always refused, much to his amusement.

"She is a queen. A dainty little queen, Sahib," he would say and the men would laugh loudly above her head. She could never understand what she had done to make them so jolly and happy.

She stopped the car and got out. What was the harm in eating a few sweets? It was Diwali after all, a religious festival to honour Goddess Laxmi. She should eat something sweet, a small laddoo maybe, just to please the Goddess.

To lose the extra 15 pounds you are carrying, you must eat 15 x 3,500 calories less than your body uses, the book advised in her head, but she quickly turned a deaf ear. Just a small piece of burfi, maybe. In fact she must eat a sweet right now. It would be inauspicious if she did not eat any mithai on Diwali. Who knows what evil might befall her if she did not follow the pattern of Diwali celebrations. Sweets. Diyas. Pooja. Sweets. Ajay may run off with the skinny one or, worse still, her boys might come to some harm. Fail their exams or something.

Reshma quickly walked into the shop and, after fighting her way through a crowd of people busy buying sweets, she reached the table and picked up a box. People jostled her as they surged forward eagerly to pick up sweets spread out on the table. A woman standing near her with a box full of silver-coated burfi whispered in her ear, "Buy the burfi, it is really fresh." As Reshma stood surrounded by the noisy, pushing crowd and watched the array of fragrant, sugary sweets, she felt strangely happy, as if everyone around her was an old friend.

"I should not buy much—but what if friends drop by? The servants, too, expect sweets on Diwali. The diet can wait. Who diets on Diwali? Only atheists," she thought.

"What are you thinking? Just taste one, sister, taste one," cried the shopkeeper, and Reshma quickly took a burfi from his sugar-coated hands and popped it into her mouth. As the familiar sweetness of solid, creamy milk cooked with cardamoms and almonds, flooded her mouth and travelled like lightning down to her toes, she plunged her hands greedily into the tray of soft, fresh, burfi.

Ajay's car was in the garage when she drove in. Why was he home so early? Perhaps the other woman had left him. Run away with a younger, richer, thinner, unmarried man. Perhaps he had had a mild heart attack at the office—afraid and guilty that he would die a sinner, he had rushed home to beg her forgiveness. Perhaps he had suddenly looked at the slim clock on his desk, which she had given him for his birthday, and realised how much he loved her, even though she *was* getting a little fat, and had come home with a present to tell her. Reshma walked into the house, carrying the boxes of sweets, and saw her husband's coat thrown across the chair. She could hear his voice in the next room shouting over the phone. She panicked suddenly and ran to hide the boxes in the cupboard just as Raha came out of the kitchen. They looked at each other and then Raha, shutting the cupboard door with a soft click, asked her if she wanted some tea.

"Why does she want to be thin? Why do they both want to be thin?" Raha asked Amah as they sat in the courtyard shelling peas. "Look at Sahib. Running on the road every morning as if a mad dog was chasing him. People might think there was a fire in his house and run behind him," said Raha. "Memsahib starves all day and then she goes and buys a mountain of sweets. She jumps about like a circus acrobat on our heads to become thin. Why do they want to be like scarecrows? Rich, healthy people like them," he asked. "When you finally make some money where else should it show but on your stomach?" he patted his soft paunch with affection.

"In my village the pujari's wife weighed as much as three sacks of grain. She could drink a full glass of ghee in one gulp. We all wanted to be like her—a goddess with a full moon face, three mighty chins and an ample, soft belly where children could play hide and seek," said Amah. "You know, I think they are afraid to look old," she added as an afterthought. Raha shook his head.

"But when you are old you should look old," he said. "People respect you then, touch your feet. When I was a young boy all I got was slaps from my father and uncles. They would box my ears for no reason whenever they passed by me. All day long I was ordered about to fetch this, fetch that. 'Send him to the well. . . to the cowshed. . . to the fields. . . to the market. . . he is the youngest.' I slept in the smallest room in our house, near the cowshed, with my brothers. We only got to eat after my grandfather, father and uncles had eaten. Sometimes my mother added water to the dal because there was not enough left for all of us. 'They are grown men. They need the food more than you young lads,' she said if I complained. I could not wait to grow old. Now everyone treats me with respect. No one dare raise his voice to me and even Sahib and Memsahib say *aap* to me," said Raha with a satisfied sigh. "In the vegetable market, the shopkeepers serve me first and the young lads later. I would never want to be young again," he added and Amah nodded her head.

She was happy to be old, too, because now she was safe. Men in the households she worked in left her alone now, and she could sleep at night with the doors open. It had taken taken a long time to grow old. So many years of fighting off groping, pinching hands in the kitchens and corridors of the many houses she had lived in. If you complained to the memsahibs they did not like it and looked at you with suspicion, as if you were to blame. Sometimes even the sahibs would brush against her when she was making the beds or sweeping the floor. Once a man, a guest in the house she was working in, came out of the bathroom and stood in front of her in a towel.

"Dry my back," he had ordered, grinning at her like an ape with black, curly hair all over his body. She had run out of the room, crying.

Yes, it was good to be old at last with a scrawny, wrinkled face. Everyone called you *amah*. Men were kinder to you and memsahibs liked you better.

In 30 days you will have reduced 11 pounds because you have reduced your intake by 39,000 calories. Stick to the same 1,000 calories for another 10-15 days and you will reach your desired weight of 128 pounds.

Reshma put the book down and reached for another burfi. She could hear Ajay singing in the bathroom. His suitcase lay packed on the bed.

"I'm going away for the weekend. A conference has suddenly come up. I wanted to send Ahuja but he can't get away because his wife is ill or something," he explained hurriedly, and Reshma knew he was lying as usual. Skinny was going with him obviously, because he had packed a new set of Marks and Spencer underwear. They lay on top of the suitcase, next to the files, their bright blue colours brazenly announcing her husband's infidelity. "I'll be back on Diwali evening. We'll go to wish Mummy and Dad," he said and kissed her on the forehead. Then, with a quick, playful slap on her bottom which resounded all over the bedroom like a dolphin's belly flip, he left the room.

"He has gone with her forever!" she wailed into the phone, twisting the cord in her hands.

"Listen, you idiot, he'll never leave you. They never do. They're afraid of what their mothers will say. Can you imagine Ajay bringing that woman to your mother-in-law's house? He doesn't even smoke in that house," said Mimi.

"But my father-in-law might take her in. He loves young women," said Reshma with a sob. She had a sudden vision of Ajay and his new wife being welcomed by his father. Ajay held a cigarette in his fingers and was blowing smoke rings into his mother's face.

"Come to the health club, you will feel better at once," enthused Mimi. "They are getting a hypnotist again today. You know the chap. . . Swami something or other. He's incredible. He can train your mind to stop eating. He looks at you for thirty seconds with his great, black eyes, Omar Sharif type, and whoosh! . . . the desire to eat vanishes. You start thinking of higher things like. . . you know, poor people, philosophy and all that sort of thing," she finished.

Reshma picked up another burfi and said, "Does he make you do social work? I don't feel strong enough these days, what with this low calorie diet."

"No. . . you don't have to do anything. Just close your eyes and think about higher things. Sonia lost five kilos in fifteen days, though her breasts sag a bit now."

Reshma touched her own heavy bosom, lifting it a little with both hands. "Yes. . . yes. I'll come," she said as she chewed the sweet slowly, letting the sugary softness cling to the corners of her mouth.

Diwali arrived. Ajay called to say he would be late.

"Don't wait for me. Go on to Mummy's. I will meet you there," he said over the telephone, his voice brimming with happiness. Reshma tried to forget the joy in his voice as she drank a glass of juice and did her exercises. Since the health club was closed and Mimi was busy with her family, Reshma had nothing to do.

"I won't think of him with her. I won't think of eating. . . or food, or sweets," Reshma chanted to herself as she walked around the house aimlessly for a while, avoiding the cupboard where the boxes of mithai were kept. She tried to remember what the hypnotist had told her but all she could remember was that he had long white hair growing out of his nostrils. "I'll do a bit of cleaning. After all, it is Diwali today," she thought and then picking up a brand new duster, she began to search the tables and chairs for dust. The house was empty and next door she could hear firecrackers exploding.

The boys could have come home from school if only Ajay had gone to fetch them. Raha had gone home to his family, catching a bus early this morning. Amah was in the kitchen making prasad for the pooja she was going to do in the evening. The fragrance of crushed cardamoms followed her around the house as Reshma tried to find something to clean. There was patch of dust on the bookshelf and she pounced on it greedily, flapping the duster about.

"Just don't think of sweets or food. Block your mind. You can have a good helping after the pooja," she told herself, like a mother placating her child. The kitchen and the dining room where the cupboard of sweets was, had now become enemy territory. She took care to avoid it, circling the rest of the house with slow, measured footsteps to pass the time. Perhaps she should exercise once more, but that would make her more hungry. No, it was better to sit down and stay still, maybe watch T.V. But all the programmes today would show people celebrating, eating sweets; shops selling sweets; women preparing sweets for their husbands and children. Reshma sat on her bed, picked up her calorie counting book and a sudden picture of Ajay and her sons loomed up. She closed the book, threw it on the floor and burst into tears.

It was dark when Amah found her. The house glittered with the diyas Amah had put all over the terrace wall. All day she had rolled hundreds of tiny wicks out of cotton wool, and placed them one by one in diyas filled with mustard oil. When the sun set, she had finished her pooja and lit the lamps. Now only the ones which lined the driveway were left. Those she wanted Memsahib to light. The sky was painted gold and silver as firecrackers shot up one after the other, leaving a trail of smoke. Stars of fire burst all around them and Amah put her hands over her ears as a bomb went off next door. Sahib had still not returned and Memsahib was fast asleep, the light from the firecrackers streaking crazily across her face. The room was in darkness but Amah spied Memsahib's book lying on the floor, its pages torn and crumpled.

She wiped the plate clean with the last bit of paratha and then took another one from the huge pile. This one was made of cauliflower. Reshma chewed slowly, and as she ate she could see the fat from her body melting away like water from an ice cube. As the stream of fat formed a pool on the bedroom floor it made a lovely pattern of leaves. Reshma patted her thin stomach and picked up a bowl of dal makhni. There was no spoon so she just drank it down in one gulp. Then she reached for the mattar samosas, throwing them one after the other into her mouth, like a juggler. All around her were bowls of kheer and halwa, mountains of burfi, laddoo, cashews, almonds, and rasmalai. The fat ran faster now and as her body shrank, she rose into the air. In the noisy firework display that followed, Ajay cheered and lifted her in his arms. He threw her up high in the air like a child and caught her again. She laughed loudly and opened her eyes. Amah was shaking her arm.

"I have brought some prasad for you," she said and proffered a plate of gleaming halwa.

Reshma sat up and snatched the plate from Amah's hands. Stuffing her mouth greedily with the sweet, greasy halwa, she finished it, then threw the plate away. A reckless madness swept through her. She caught Amah by the waist.

"Diwali! Diwali! Let's go and celebrate!" she shouted like a child. Dressed only in her petticoat and blouse, Reshma dragged Amah behind her into the dining room. She flung open the cupboard and took the boxes out.

"Let us eat, Amah, eat. . . eat. . . eat!" she shouted and grabbed a handful of laddoos. She stuffed them into her mouth and then forced some into Amah's hands. Clutching the box, she ran into the kitchen. Picking up the bowl of halwa and using her cupped fingers as a spoon, she began to eat. "Come on, Amah, come on. Take some. Don't be afraid. We can never become fat. It is Diwali. Let us eat. . . eat. . . eat. . .," she laughed and covered her ears as a cracker went off somewhere nearby.

Reshma ate all the sweets in the boxes and then began to bring out all the bowls of leftover food she found in the fridge. She forced Amah to eat with her and made her sit at the table. Amah could not look at her and kept her head bowed. Reshma ran up and brought some chocolates from her bedroom. Amah did not like the taste of chocolate. These had a stale brown liquid in them, but she ate one so that Memsahib would not get angry. Amah had never seen her like this and felt a little bewildered.

After an hour of eating whatever she could find, including sugar from the sugar bowl, Reshma suddenly stopped and began to cry soundlessly. Amah did not know what to do. She wanted to touch her, hold her hand but she was afraid to. As Reshma sat, tears flowing, Amah began to cut a piece of fresh ginger into fine bits to make ginger tea. She put in ground cardamoms and cloves and then added milk and four spoons of sugar. Two spoons for each of them. Reshma watched her as she stirred the tea slowly with a long spoon, letting it simmer. Gradually, as the tea began to boil, she stopped crying. She sat still like a ragdoll, slumped on the chair, picking bits of leftover laddoo off her blouse. They could hear firecrackers outside and an occasional silver star fell across the garden. Amah sang tunelessly as they sipped the sweet ginger tea.

Pink as a lotus; plump as the full moon;
Smile, my little angel, and I will cook you almond kheer.

ORANGE KHEER

2 litres milk

100 gm khoya

2 cups orange segments

½ cup sugar

Boil the milk to reduce it to half. Add sugar and stir. Mix in khoya and take off the fire. When cool add the orange segments. Chill, decorate with strips of fine orange rind and serve. For variations on the kheer theme, instead of oranges add small rasgullas bought from a halwai. Or, before taking off the fire, add 100 gms of ground, peeled almonds for a delicious almond kheer.

HOT GINGER–HONEY DRINK

Take five finely cut pieces of fresh ginger, five basil (tulsi) leaves, five cloves, five whole peppercorns and one small cardamom. Boil the spices and ginger in two cups of water. Simmer slowly till the mixture turns light brown and the water is reduced to almost half. Add one teaspoon of honey and sip slowly, inhaling the lovely aroma. This brew is my cure for everything, from coughs and colds to heartache and hunger pangs.

Index of Recipes